"Why don't you just accept the inevitable?" he sneered. **"You've made my life more difficult, but you can't escape your fate."**

She suddenly spied a crowbar among the hay and dirt on the ground and reached to grab it, then turned to face him. *God, please help me!* she prayed silently. He was only about ten feet away now. She knew she probably wouldn't win this battle, but she was going to go down fighting. And she knew God was with her. Her terror was starting to ebb, and was replaced with an intense fierceness that strengthened her resolve. Regardless of how this turned out, she knew she wasn't alone.

"I don't believe in fate. God is with me." She brandished the crowbar, even as he approached her.

"You think that little piece of metal is going to stop me?" he said, his voice rough and odious. "I always liked a challenge. Keep on fighting me. It will make everything more fun." He took a step toward her...

Kathleen Tailer is a senior attorney II who works for the Supreme Court of Florida in the office of the state courts administrator. She graduated from Florida State University College of Law after earning her BA from the University of New Mexico. She and her husband have eight children, five of whom they adopted from the state of Florida. She enjoys photography and playing drums on the worship team at Calvary Chapel in Thomasville, Georgia.

Books by Kathleen Tailer

Love Inspired Suspense

Visit the Author Profile page at LoveInspired.com.

MARKED TO DIE

KATHLEEN TAILER

LOVE INSPIRED SUSPENSE

INSPIRATIONAL ROMANCE

LOVE INSPIRED® SUSPENSE
INSPIRATIONAL ROMANCE

ISBN-13: 978-1-335-59772-4

Recycling programs for this product may not exist in your area.

Marked to Die

For questions and comments about the quality of this book, please contact us at CustomerService@Harlequin.com.

Love Inspired
22 Adelaide St. West, 41st Floor
Toronto, Ontario M5H 4E3, Canada
www.LoveInspired.com

Printed in U.S.A.

And let us not be weary in well doing:
for in due season we shall reap, if we faint not.
—*Galatians* 6:9

For my wonderful and ever-growing family:
James, Bethany, Daniel, Keandra, Bryon, Joshua,
Bradley, Brayden, B.J., Jessica, Nathan, Anna and Megan,
and for my precious son, Joshua Evan Tailer, who died
on April 23, 2022, at the age of 23. We miss you so much
and will love you forever. You are with Jesus now, but
never forgotten!

Also, for all of my wonderful readers: Thank you for
spending your time with me! I am honored that you
picked up my book. I hope you have as much fun reading
it as I did writing it. May God bless you!

ONE

"Look, Mama, that woman over there fell down!" Katie's five-year-old voice reached Eleni Townsend's ears and quickly pulled her out of her woolgathering. It had been a stressful day, and she was still running through her afternoon agenda in her head, but her daughter's words penetrated her musings and she quickly focused on what was going on around them. She followed her daughter's pointing finger and gasped as she saw not one but two adults stagger and fall to the ground. Both had been standing at a table and eating their lunch beneath colorful red and blue umbrellas. The city had recently added them to the plaza so workers from the nearby buildings could grab a bite from the local restaurants before returning to work.

"Help...please..." A third man who had been sitting on a large concrete flower planter while enjoying his lunch suddenly grabbed his head. He moaned and then started convulsing, his arms and legs flailing as he, too, tumbled to the concrete. He suddenly started gasping for air and clutching at his throat, and all three of the affected adults' faces and hands started to turn a bright cherry red. As the third man fell, he knocked over the Styrofoam container of salad that he had been enjoying. Tomatoes, lettuce and purple cabbage went flying, as well as the bag from Marino's Deli that advertised where he had no doubt bought his lunch.

Chaos ensued. Several nearby people screamed, while others ran across the plaza, unsure of the threat but still trying to get to safety as if there was an active shooter, despite the fact that no gunshots had sounded. A brave few tried to help the people who had fallen.

Marino's Deli? Time suddenly seemed to stand still as Eleni took in the scene around her. A cold sweat swept over her as she looked at her own lunch that she and her daughter had just purchased from Marino's. Her own Styrofoam container hadn't been opened yet, but her daughter's salad filled with the purple cabbage and other salad fixings she loved so much was open, and her daughter had already taken two or three bites from her perch on the picnic table. She looked closer at her daughter. Katie's skin was suddenly flushed and turning redder right before her eyes, and the faint scent of almonds permeated the air.

"Mama, I feel yucky," Katie said softly. She put her little hands up to her throat and was suddenly struggling for air. "I can't breathe very good."

Eleni pulled out her phone and immediately dialed 911, at the same time pushing her daughter's food across the table as far away as possible and then pulling her daughter into her arms.

"911. What's the nature of your emergency?"

"My daughter can't breathe, and others are getting sick and falling down in the Southern Plaza in downtown Chicago near the river." She glanced around the scene. "There are at least three others, no, make that five other people, that are all getting sick. We need help immediately!" She struggled to keep the fear out of her voice and speak coherently, but her heart was beating so loudly it seemed to drown out her words. Her throat felt dry and she swallowed convulsively.

"Do you know CPR?" the woman asked from the other end of the phone.

"Yes, but my training was a while ago," Eleni replied in a raspy voice.

"Okay. I'll walk you through it if it turns out you need to do it. Just stay on the line. Help is on the way. I'm sending emergency personnel to your location while we're speaking."

Panic swelled inside Eleni's chest as she lay Katie down on the concrete and loosened the buttons on her child's jacket. She'd lost her husband only a year ago. She couldn't lose Katie, too. Her daughter was everything to her. The little girl started gasping for breath, and her face and hands had gotten even redder. The child's big gray eyes were rounded in fear, and Eleni's hands shook as she tried to help her daughter stay calm. "You're going to be okay, Katie. Just lie here and concentrate on your breathing. Help is coming." She tried to keep her voice even and soft, despite the terror that was surging within her. "That's good. You're doing great, Katie. I'm talking to a woman on the phone who has already sent someone to help. She's telling me what to do so I can help you."

Katie nodded, but suddenly reached over and grasped Eleni's hand and held on tightly. Eleni could tell that each breath was labored, but thankfully, the little girl hadn't lost consciousness or gone into convulsions like a couple of the nearby adults. The mere thought of Katie's condition worsening like what was happening around them sent chills of fear throughout Eleni's entire body. She was poised and ready to do CPR if needed, but so far, it wasn't required. Even though Katie was struggling, she was still breathing on her own and conscious. Eleni immediately started to pray in a soft soothing tone that only she and her daughter could hear.

"Dear God, please save my daughter. Please help her breathe, and stop whatever is going on inside her so she can get well. Please help the medical people get here quickly so they can help Katie and the others who are also sick. Please help her stay calm, and know that You are with her always. Strengthen her, Lord. Amen."

Emergency medical personnel and law enforcement arrived shortly and immediately spread out among the victims, helping who they could and keeping the crowds away that had started forming around the edges of the plaza. Eleni barely noticed them as she kept her focus on her daughter. She wanted to do everything she could to make sure her little girl was as comfortable as possible. A female EMT with kind brown eyes knelt next to Eleni and immediately began assessing Katie. She called for a gurney, and before Eleni even registered what was happening, they were both ensconced in an ambulance, being whisked away to the nearest hospital with the sirens blazing. A small oxygen mask had been strapped over Katie's mouth, and the child seemed to already be breathing a little better. The EMT continued to monitor Katie's blood pressure and heart rate as the ambulance raced toward its destination.

"Any history of breathing problems?" the EMT asked.

"None," Eleni replied as she squeezed Katie's small hand. "She's up-to-date on all of her immunizations and is hardly ever sick."

"Can you tell me what happened today?"

"We were just getting ready to eat our lunch like we do every weekday, when Katie noticed some of the other people around us getting ill. Then she started having trouble breathing, too." She studied Katie carefully, who was much less agitated now that the oxygen was getting into her system. It was hard not to exhibit the anxiety she was feeling inside, but Eleni knew she had to stay calm for her daughter's sake. Katie still held her hand, but her grip had loosened. Eleni gave Katie's hand a squeeze and met the EMT's eye. "Any idea what's going on here?"

"We'll have to run some tests," the woman hedged. "The doctors at the hospital can give you better answers once they have a handle on what's going on."

"Do you think it's food poisoning?"

"I doubt it," the EMT responded, shaking her head.

"The symptoms are wrong. First of all, food poisoning usually takes a lot longer to affect the victim, but it also almost always causes nausea, vomiting and stomach cramps." She fiddled with a dial on one of the machines.

"Are the others who were affected okay?"

"Not yet. Most are in transit to either the same hospital where we're going or headed to Rush University Medical Center. There was a huge traffic accident nearby, so ambulances are getting diverted to different locations."

A few minutes later, Katie had been transferred to a hospital bed in the emergency room, and a young female doctor was standing by her bedside and reviewing her chart. The doctor had beautiful warm brown skin and dark brown eyes that were shrewd and accessing. She exuded a quiet strength and confidence, and Eleni found her presence alone incredibly reassuring. This woman clearly knew what she was doing.

"Hi. I'm Dr. McNeill. What have we got here?" the doctor asked as she set the chart aside and turned her full attention to the child who was laid out on the bed before her.

"I started eating lunch and then couldn't breathe very good," Katie offered. "Then my skin started turning all red. See?" She held up her hands toward the doctor.

"Ah," the doctor said as she took Katie's hands and gave them a squeeze. "Well, it sounds like you're breathing a little better now. Is that right?"

Katie nodded and Eleni explained what had happened, and then gave the doctor time to check her daughter's other symptoms. Katie behaved well and answered the doctor's questions during the examination, and was rewarded with a kind smile and a pat on the leg.

"Do you know what's wrong with her?" Eleni asked once the doctor had finished.

"My first thought is cyanide poisoning," Dr. McNeill replied. "That would explain the red skin tone, respiratory problems and that faint almond smell." She gave Katie a reassuring smile. "Cyanide exposure can cause heart problems, like cardiac arrest, but Katie's heart is doing great. We'll know more about what we're dealing with once the blood tests come back. For your daughter, it looks like her exposure was not as severe as what some of the others are experiencing, and I think she'll be fine once the poison works its way out of her system. I'd like to keep her here for a few hours for observation, though."

"Of course," Eleni readily agreed. "How in the world would she get cyanide poisoning?"

"That I couldn't tell you," Dr. McNeill replied. "Although I believe law enforcement is investigating, and will be in touch—probably even before you leave the hospital. It's not something we see very often." She gave Katie another smile and squeezed her hand. "I'll return in a few minutes once the test results come back. In the meantime, just rest. You're going to be okay." She left, leaving Eleni with her mind full of questions.

Cyanide poisoning? Who would do such a terrible

thing, and how had her five-year-old daughter been exposed? Before she had a chance to think through the possibilities, a large man wearing a navy suit with a silver tie poked his head around the hospital curtain. He was tall, well over six feet, and had broad shoulders like a linebacker. His blond hair was cut short, in a military style, and he had pale blue eyes. In Eleni's mind, he was obviously law enforcement from his demeanor and bearing.

"Eleni and Katie Townsend?" he asked.

"Yes, that's right," Eleni responded.

"I'm Chris Springfield, FBI. I wanted to talk to you about what happened downtown today." He glanced at Katie and his manner suddenly changed from friendly to nervous in two seconds flat. He adjusted quickly and gave Katie a wide smile, even though Eleni could tell it was forced. "You doing okay, short stuff?"

Katie smiled up at him and Eleni was instantly glad this man took the time to greet her daughter, even though it was obvious that something was bothering him about the encounter. She'd dealt with several law enforcement officers when her husband had died last year after a horrible car crash, but they had been all business and similar to the "just the facts, ma'am" persona from the old TV shows. It was refreshing to see that this officer made the effort to put Katie a little more at ease, even though it cost him something personally.

She took his measure from head to toe. His shoes were polished to a high gloss, and he sported a small American flag tiepin and a military-style watch. His size and demeanor simply exuded authority, and he seemed professional yet a bit daunting at the same time. When he smiled, however, everything changed. His imposing visage softened, and he seemed approachable, even friendly. She glanced at his eyes, which were amicable but also intelligent and perceptive. She doubted he missed much with those eyes, and was instantly glad that he had been assigned to this case. She wanted answers, and this man just might be able to get them for her. Who had hurt her little girl? And why?

"Care to step away for a few minutes while I ask you some questions?" Chris Springfield motioned with his head toward the hallway to the mother who was hovering protectively over her daughter. His gut had tightened the instant he'd discovered that a child was involved in this case, and now that he'd seen the child's big gray eyes with the dark lashes, his wariness had increased tenfold. His last case had just about destroyed him. An eight-year-old girl had been kidnapped and killed, and he had been helpless to stop it. He wasn't sure he was strong enough to handle another case involving a child, but orders were orders. For now, and until he decided on a different course for his life, he had no choice but to investigate this case and do his utmost to solve it before another person was harmed, especially this precious little girl before him.

Eleni raised an eyebrow, but seemed to understand his motive behind talking in private. She turned to the child. "Katie, you stay here and rest, okay? I'm going to go down the hall for a few minutes and talk to this nice FBI agent. I won't be very long."

The child nodded and Eleni sent her a comforting smile, then followed Chris to a nearby alcove that housed a coffeepot and a box of stale doughnuts as well as several employee lockers. Chris motioned to a green vinyl chair while he took the one on the other side of a small Formica table. "Have a seat, Ms. Townsend." Although the space wasn't very private, it was in a corner that had less traffic than the main hall, and was away from Katie's little ears. It would do for now. Chris took the seat with his back facing the row of lockers, which allowed him to surveil the surrounding area.

The woman complied as he pulled out his phone and got ready to take notes on an app. She looked somewhat familiar to him, but he couldn't quite place her. "So, again, my name is Chris Springfield, and I work with the FBI as a member of a team of homicide special agents that get pulled in when we have an unusual case that needs our expertise. Our jurisdiction in this case exists because of suspected terrorism." He paused, giving her time to let that sink in. "It looks like Katie is doing great, but we did have seven other people that were also hurt today, and five of those people died."

Eleni gasped and covered her mouth with her hand, obviously upset. "Those poor people. I'm so sorry to hear that."

Chris nodded and pushed forward. "Can you tell

me what happened out there? We're still trying to piece everything together, and every detail matters, even if it's small and you don't think it's important. If you don't mind, please start with when you left your house this morning, and go through everything you've done today until I just popped my head in from behind the hospital curtain and said hello."

Eleni took a deep breath. "My daughter, Katie, is five, and she does better with a routine, so we basically do the same thing every day during the week. Today was no exception. We got up at about seven, had breakfast, got ready to go and grabbed the 'L.' We took the blue line at Irving Park station and rode into the downtown area. I dropped her off at about 8:15 at her kindergarten class at the church on Grand, and then I went to work in the building on the corner of Illinois and North Park. You know, the one they're renovating?"

"Sure. Okay. So, what do you do?"

"I'm an investigative reporter for the *Chicago Journal*."

Chris cringed inside, but did his best to keep his feelings from showing. It was just his luck to be interviewing a reporter. As a group, they were just about his least favorite people on the planet. A few years ago, he'd been burned by a reporter who had misquoted him in an article. As a result, a person had been unfairly victimized who hadn't actually been involved in the original nasty situation. Even though it wasn't his fault, he still carried the guilt around with him today. The paper had printed a retraction, but it was too little, too late, and the person still had a lingering limp as a result of the violence that had ensued. Of course, the woman in front of him had nothing to do with that affair, but her profession still bothered him. He shifted in his chair, hoping his uncomfortable response wasn't too evident. These days, he was having a hard time masking his feelings. "Okay. Then what?"

Eleni shrugged. "I worked until noon, then went and picked up Katie for lunch. We do the same thing every weekday. We leave her school at about 12:05, and then we walk to Marino's and get a salad. Then we take our food to the plaza if the weather is good, we talk about our day and I take her back to school at one o'clock. After lunch, I go back to work, and pick Katie up at a few minutes past five to head home again."

Chris's fingers flew as he wrote down more notes on the app on his phone. "Okay. Do you eat the same food at Marino's every day? You said you get a salad."

Eleni shrugged. "Pretty much. Katie and I are both vegetarians, so the salad bar works for us, and is one of the best lunch options downtown. Plus, the owner is the father of a friend of mine, and he gives me a great discount. We eat there so much, we have a running tab and pay by the month." She tilted her head. "Do you think there was poison on the food? Mr. Marino is a sweetheart and would never be involved in anything that would hurt anyone. I'm sure he's a victim here just like everyone else. I hope this incident doesn't destroy his business."

"Poison is one theory. The doctors think it might be cyanide, which means it was placed on the food deliberately. So far, the restaurant is the only common factor we've found between the victims, but we're still investigating, and it's early yet. I have several more interviews to conduct."

Eleni's face paled right before him and even though she tried to hide her hands, he could still see them shaking violently. "So, someone intentionally tried to kill us?"

"Yes, it seems intentional. We don't know who the intended victim was yet, or if this was just a random act of terrorism. We're also still waiting for the labs to confirm the form of cyanide used." He leaned forward. "Did you eat any of your food from the restaurant?"

Eleni shook her head. "No. We were just getting settled. Katie took a couple of bites, and that's when she noticed the people starting to struggle around us. I never even opened my lunch."

Chris nodded thoughtfully, still taking notes. "Do you have any enemies, Ms. Townsend?"

Just then, a child's scream echoed through the emergency room, and Eleni jumped to her feet. "That's Katie!" She darted back down the hall and Chris followed close behind.

Had somebody just finished what they'd tried to accomplish with the cyanide poisoning earlier today?

Had the child been the intended victim all along?

TWO

Eleni saw the back of a man with short dark hair and a navy jacket disappearing quickly down the hallway, but everything else going on around her seemed normal for a hospital emergency room. Why was that man rushing away? Had he been the one behind the curtain who had scared her daughter? She couldn't tell exactly where he had come from, or what he really looked like, since she had only gotten a glimpse of his face. Part of her wanted to chase the man down and find out, but instead, she stayed rooted in place and focused on Katie. She pulled back the curtain and heaved a giant sigh of relief when she saw that her daughter was still lying down in her hospital bed just as she'd left her, no worse for wear. "Katie! What happened? Are you okay?"

The little girl's features crumpled as soon as she saw her mom. "Mommy, there was a man here who scared me! He touched my arm, but he was a stranger so I yelled like you told me to! I didn't want him to touch me."

"Did he work for the hospital?" Eleni asked.

"No, he wasn't wearing doctor clothes," Katie responded with tears in her eyes.

Eleni gathered her daughter up in her arms, careful to avoid the IV and oxygen lines, and sat with her on the bed. The child had already been terrified at the plaza when the adults had all been yelling and rushing around, and her ride in the ambulance with an oxygen mask on her face had also been stressful. She was only five years old, after all. Their normal routine had totally been shattered today, and not in a good way. It wasn't surprising that she'd been scared by a stranger, even if his actions had been totally innocuous. "You did just the right thing, Katydid," Eleni said in a reassuring tone, using the pet name she'd used for the little girl ever since she had started walking. Katie had a habit of bouncing around, just like the grasshopper. "I'm so proud of you." She hugged the small girl while also surreptitiously checking her over for injuries. "Did he hurt you?"

"No. He was just really scary. I didn't want him to touch me, so I yelled."

"I think that was a really good idea." Eleni caught the girl's eye. "Did he say anything to you?"

"He just asked me if my name was Katie, and when I said yes, he didn't smile and looked kind of scary, like he was mad or something."

"What did he look like?" The voice came from behind her, and Eleni turned slightly to see that the burly FBI agent had followed her and was now standing directly behind her.

"I don't know," Katie said softly.

"Well, was his skin color white like me, dark brown like Dr. McNeill or light brown?" Chris urged.

Katie thought for a minute and tapped her chin with a finger. "He looked like you, but his hair wasn't like yours, and he wasn't big like you."

"Was his hair dark like yours, or a different color?"

"Dark. Kind of like mine and Mama's."

"Did he have any hair on his face, like a mustache or a beard?"

The little girl shook her head.

"Wow, Katie. You're doing a really good job of answering my questions," Chris said with a wink. "Do you remember what color his clothes were?"

Katie was silent for a minute and tilted her head to the right, then pointed at the agent's chest. "Blue, I think. Like your jacket, but he didn't have a tie."

"I saw a white man with dark hair and a navy jacket speeding down the hallway right after she yelled. It might have been him," Eleni offered. "He looked like he came out of this area, but I wasn't sure." She turned to her daughter. "Katie, was the man wearing a blue jacket that was kind of shiny, like your soccer uniform?" The little girl nodded and Chris turned abruptly and quickly disappeared. Eleni assumed he was going after the man, but wanted to make sure security was notified anyway. She sat Katie back on the bed, then pulled open the curtain and motioned to a passing nurse and asked her to report the incident to the hospital's security team. The nurse promised to let security know, so Eleni went back to Katie's side and pulled the curtain closed again. The drape was only a thick piece of fabric, but for some reason, it made her feel just a little bit safer to have it circling Katie's bed and giving them a touch of privacy.

Eleni didn't understand what was happening, and she felt a large knot twist in her stomach. Why would anyone want to hurt Katie? She took the child's hand and gave it a reassuring squeeze. Katie was a pretty little girl with chocolate brown hair and large gray eyes, and she was missing her front tooth and had a beautiful gap-toothed smile. But even though Eleni thought she was incredibly special and loved her unconditionally, there were hundreds if not thousands of other similar children in Chicago. Why would anyone want to hurt Katie in particular? Why had she been singled out? Was today's attack in the plaza truly random, or part of something bigger? There had to be a different answer. Katie must have been collateral damage from some different scheme. If not, none of this made any sense.

Eleni rubbed her neck with her fingers, trying to ease the stress out of her muscles. Questions rushed through her brain, one on top of another. Her husband, Charlie, had died a year ago in a horrible car crash. Even though law enforcement had disagreed, Eleni was convinced that someone had killed him deliberately by forcing his car off the road. But that tragedy had occurred almost a year ago. Could Charlie's death and today's attack be linked, even though a year had passed? Or was she seeing conspiracies where they didn't exist? What about the other victims? Had one of them been the actual target?

Before she could come up with any feasible ideas, the FBI agent had returned. He wasn't breathing hard, but his face was flushed, and it was obvious he had been running. "Did you find him?" Eleni asked hopefully.

Chris shook his head. "No, I got a glimpse of him, but he left through the emergency room bay doors, which lead out to the sidewalk, and it was pretty crowded. He's long gone now. I checked with security about the hospital cameras, but they didn't catch him outside, and inside, they don't allow cameras due to federal privacy laws."

Eleni let her shoulders slump. "I can't figure this out. Why would anyone want to hurt all those people at the restaurant, or try to bother Katie here at the hospital?"

"Well, despite what just happened here with the man in blue, we don't know which of the victims, if any, were actually the targets of the poison. It could have even been a random act of violence committed by a terrorist group. It's just too soon to say. What I would like is to get your information so I can contact you as the investigation progresses. I may have more questions."

"Of course," Eleni agreed as she shared her email address, home address and phone number. She rubbed her arms, trying to warm up after a cold chill had once again swept over her from head to toe.

Chris stored the information in his phone, doing his best to hide the feelings of stress that were rushing over him in waves. He took another step away from the child, hoping his discomfort wasn't obvious.

Why did a little girl have to be involved in this case?

For over five years, Chris had been part of an elite section of the FBI that focused on unusual homicide cases, but the last investigation he had handled had almost been his undoing. An eight-year-old girl had been kidnapped from a summer day-camp program right here in Chicago. Although his team had done everything possible to save her and return her to her family, the girl had been murdered. Unfortunately, he had also been the one to find the child's broken and battered body. To this day, the visions from that horrible scene kept seeping into his nightmares. Even during the daylight hours, he was haunted by the memories of the day he had discovered her. Unfortunately, the small child sitting on the hospital bed in front of him was a stark reminder of the victim from the previous case. The child's hair was the same color, and they had a similar build, even though the little girl before him was younger. Chris's palms got sweaty every time he looked at Katie Townsend, and small beads of perspiration popped out on his forehead as well.

Was this visceral reaction going to happen every time the victim in the case was a child? If so, how could he continue to do his job properly? Could he even stay in law enforcement? Doubts assailed him as he took yet another step away from the child. Her big gray eyes glanced his direction, but thankfully, neither she nor her mother seemed aware of his problems. He wanted to keep it that way. A quick exit was in order.

"Alright, Ms. Townsend, I'll be in touch if we learn anything more. In the meantime, please be aware of your surroundings at all times, lock your doors and if possible, try to vary your usual routine."

He was about to turn and leave when recognition finally dawned. He knew he'd seen the mother somewhere before. Her features were hard to forget. "Wait a minute. Are you the Eleni Townsend that did an exposé on that investment scheme that's been in the news for the last few weeks?"

Eleni raised an eyebrow. "Yes, that was me."

All of the uncomfortable feelings that Chris had been experiencing suddenly doubled. If the stories about her were true, this woman was a bulldog. Her reporting had resulted in the arrests of several powerful people that had been involved in the financial scheme she'd uncovered, and she'd also garnered the reputation of being relentless and tough as nails. That hard-hitting status might help when it came to ferreting out the truth about a financial crime, but he wondered if she was going to make his FBI job even harder than in already was. Eleni Townsend didn't quit. Ever. That was a great trait in a reporter, but not such a great trait in a victim. Personalities and working styles aside, however, the fact that she was involved in such a highly visible case brought a brand-new wrinkle to his investigation. Was she the intended victim in this poisoning because of her report? It was certainly a possibility that needed exploring.

"How did you hear about it?" Eleni asked.

Chris raised an eyebrow. "You're kidding, right? You ruffled a lot of feathers with that investigation. It was all over the news, and my office. I think you'd be hard-pressed to find someone who *hasn't* heard about it."

Eleni frowned. "Is that a bad thing? I uncovered massive corruption that needed to be prosecuted. You sound like that bothers you."

"Not at all. In fact, I'm impressed with all of the arrests that came as a result of your story. I'm just wondering if that case has anything to do with today's events."

Eleni blew out a breath. "I was actually wondering the same thing, but that story broke over a month ago." She brushed some of the hair out of Katie's eyes and gave her small leg a comforting pat. "And there's something else you should know. My husband, Charlie Townsend, was killed almost a year ago. I've been wondering if that might also be connected somehow, although I can't figure out how or why." Her hands moved to her hairline, and she rubbed her temples. "I honestly just don't know what to think."

Eleni Townsend was a very attractive woman. The revelation hit Chris like a ton of bricks. The motion with her hands drew his attention to her heart-shaped face as well as her beautiful gray eyes and fine porcelain skin. She also had a nice wide mouth with full lips, and dark brown hair with reddish highlights that cascaded to her shoulders. She was tall, probably about five-ten, and was wearing an attractive burgundy suit that was tailored perfectly to her curves. He'd been so busy dealing with his own insecurities surrounding the child that he hadn't even really noticed Eleni's attractive qualities before, but now he couldn't stop staring.

His mouth dried and he swallowed. He did *not* need to be noticing Eleni's features. What was wrong with him? His thoughts were suddenly all over the place. First this kid had sent his mind spinning, and now he was getting distracted by the looks and history of the woman before him. Maybe he did need to find a new profession. He gave himself a mental kick and tried to focus on the case at hand. He had several more people to interview, and his boss and former partner, Tessa McIntyre, would be expecting his report shortly. He needed to get moving.

"Okay, as I said, I'll be in touch. I still have to interview some of the other victims and their families as well."

He turned and quickly left the area without waiting for a response, heading to speak with the doctor that was in charge of one of the other patients from the plaza poisoning. One thing was for sure, if he was going to stay with law enforcement, he was going to have to get his head on straight and quit letting Katie remind him of the poor murdered girl from his previous case, and her mother, the tiger reporter with the pretty gray eyes.

THREE

"Can you run it back?" Chris peered at the screen, leaning forward so he could get an even better view. The FBI crime lab was fantastic, and had rushed their tests and managed to narrow down the source of the poison that had killed and injured the people in the plaza downtown. The techs had found cyanide in the purple cabbage bin in the salad bar at Marino's Deli, as suspected. Now they just had to figure out who had distributed the poison in the first place, and why.

Chris peered intently at the screen as he watched the activity near the salad bar. Did that man's hand go near the contaminated purple cabbage section? He watched again as the man on the video used the tongs to grab some mushrooms, but although he got close to the cabbage, he wasn't holding anything but the tongs, and he didn't actually touch the cabbage container or any of the vegetable slices inside. Chris sighed and shook his head. "Okay, forget it. That's not our perp. Can you fast-forward to the next person?"

Jerome Renfrew, the FBI's best computer tech and one of Chris's friends at the Bureau, hit some keys on his keyboard, then took another sip from his soda cup. "Sure thing, Chris."

The video zipped ahead a few seconds until another restaurant customer came into view on the screen. While this person took items from several of the vegetable containers, he didn't go near the cabbage either. Chris gritted his teeth in disappointment and pushed his chair back.

"That's the last one," Jerome said as he clicked some more buttons on his keyboard.

"And not a single one goes near the cabbage, which is where the lab said the poison was found."

"That's right," Jerome agreed.

Chris ran his hands through his hair in frustration. "Well, there's only one other option. Somebody tainted the food in the kitchen before it was brought out."

"Any cameras in the kitchen?"

"Nope," Chris responded.

"But what if someone poisoned it before the cabbage even made it to the kitchen?" Jerome asked, taking another sip of soda.

"We thought of that," Chris said with a shrug. "The lab tested everywhere in the kitchen. If the cyanide had come in on the cabbage, trace amounts would have also been found on the cutting board, on the knives they used to chop it or even in some of the other foods that had been prepared at the same location in Marino's kitchen. But they didn't find poison anywhere but on the cut cabbage in the container that was actually in the salad bar." He stood and started pacing. "It's hard to imagine how the perpetrator could have expected a particular victim to take the cabbage. That makes me think this was more of a terrorist act to hit random victims rather than anyone in particular."

Now it was Jerome's turn to shrug. "Unless the intended victim was such a creature of habit that they ate the same food at the same restaurant day after day." He tilted his head. "Or, the perp could want you to think that it was random to throw you off the scent. I saw a movie once where a guy took out four other people because he didn't want his motive discovered. He figured if the crime resulted in multiple victims, then the true victim, and therefore the true motive, would never be exposed."

Chris nodded, thinking he might have even seen the same movie. He glanced at the tech and gave him a smile. Despite his laid-back appearance and messy work space deep in the basement of the FBI building in Chicago, Jerome was a heavy hitter in the computer field. He could find data that users thought they had deleted years ago, and he was an absolute wonder with the keyboard. Still, it was times like these when Chris appreciated him even more. His comments about motive actually hit a chord. "You're absolutely right. I guess it's too soon to rule anything out at this point."

"Hey, Chris!"

Chris looked up the stairs that led to the floor above and saw Caitlin McPherson coming toward him. Caitlin had replaced Tessa McIntyre, his old partner, when Tessa had been promoted to special agent in charge of the Chicago office about a month ago. Caitlin was still getting her feet wet in Chicago, and had just recently transferred from Dallas into their division. They had only worked a couple of cases together so far, but she had proven herself to be smart and insightful in each of them. She had a headful of dark brown curly hair that she tried to keep tamed, but usually, as now, one curl had escaped and was hanging by her dark brown eyes and bouncing as she talked. She also had a killer smile. Even though Chris found Caitlin attractive, theirs was a purely platonic friendship. They had already been developing a good working relationship, and he was enjoying her quick wit and shrewd deductions. His feelings for Caitlin were nothing like what he had experienced when he'd interviewed Eleni. Why couldn't he get that reporter out of his mind?

Caitlin leaned over the railing and caught his eye. "Guess who's called about a dozen times this afternoon for you."

"Eleni Townsend." He'd already been given several messages from her through their administrative staff, but hadn't taken the time to return the calls yet.

"And guess who is waiting upstairs in your office."

Chris's head snapped up. "What?"

"She's determined, I'll give her that much. My guess is that she's planted herself by your desk and she's not planning on moving until she actually talks to you."

"Good grief." He turned to Jerome. "Thanks again for flipping through those videos with me."

Jerome nodded. "Sure thing."

"Ya'll find anything?" Caitlin asked in her slow Texan drawl.

"Nope," Chris answered as he headed up the stairs. "But since we didn't, we know the poison was put on the food in the kitchen after it was prepared. There were no traces anywhere else on the salad bar or in the other salad bins, and no one touched the purple cabbage but the victims. Now we'll have to focus our attention on anyone that had access to the kitchen that morning."

"Well, that's progress at least," Caitlin agreed. "We've finished our interviews with all of the kitchen staff. Nothing popped and no one admitted to anything. However, they also said no one besides staff entered the kitchen area all day, and if that's true, then our pool of possible suspects is getting smaller and smaller, and someone is lying. Now the background checks begin." She gave him a smile as he reached the door and looked over his shoulder at her. "I'd give fifty bucks to find a camera secreted away somewhere in that kitchen. Then the guessing would be over and our perp would already be behind bars."

"I'd give a hundred!" Chris declared. He motioned with his head. "Come get me in five if I haven't escaped. I have a feeling that Ms. Townsend won't leave until I give her the perp gift-wrapped."

Caitlin laughed as the door closed behind him and he navigated the hallways until he was back at his office. His team had split up the work, as they normally did whenever they had a big case. He'd been reviewing all of the video footage they could find, while others had been out doing more interviews, checking for recent cyanide purchases and performing other administrative tasks. Real investigations, he'd found, rarely followed the exciting path or the fast-paced time frames seen in most TV dramas. There was a ton of legwork to be done, and they rarely got immediate answers like the actors did in the one-hour TV shows.

He slowed as he neared the open door, and could see Eleni waiting for him, sitting across from his desk in the one and only chair available for guests in his office. She was wearing navy today, and her hair was pulled back in an attractive French braid that accented her high cheekbones and beautiful skin. He silently chastised himself for noticing as he entered his office. She was the victim—one of several—in the case he was working. Nothing more. Nothing less.

"Ms. Townsend?" She stood as he arrived, and despite his internal resolutions, he couldn't help but admire the highlights in her hair and the flash of intelligence in her gray eyes as he motioned toward the chair. "Please sit. How can I help you?" He felt a warmth suffuse him at her smile and gritted his teeth. Good grief. She was truly attractive. Why couldn't he keep his eye on the ball whenever she was around? It seemed like all of his common sense flew right out the window whenever he was around her. He really didn't like his reaction, but seemed unable to stop himself, which made him even more frustrated.

"Special Agent." She offered her hand and he shook

it quickly before pulling back and seating himself behind his desk.

She raised an eyebrow at his brusqueness, but sat down again as well and pierced him with her intense gaze. "I'm here to get an update on the case. I tried calling, but I haven't heard from you. Apparently, your phone has been off."

"Not exactly," he hedged. "But I have been working the case, which doesn't leave a lot of time for chitchat." He knew instantly that he'd offended her with his comment by the way she bristled and straightened her spine. Still, he couldn't make himself regret his words. There were only so many hours in a day, and he needed to stay focused. He would give her updates, but only when he truly had progress that he was willing and able to share with her.

"Believe me, Special Agent, when I say chitchat was the farthest thing from my mind. I need answers. It was my daughter lying in that hospital bed, and I could have been lying right beside her if I'd eaten my own lunch."

"How is Katie?" he asked, hoping to deflect her somewhat and lessen her ire. He hadn't meant to antagonize her.

"She's much better, thank you for asking. It looks like there won't be any lasting effects from the poison. She's staying with a friend for now until we can get this mess sorted out. I'm afraid to have her at home with me until we identify the perpetrator."

Chris raised his eyebrow. It was wise of her to move Katie to safety, but he didn't like the way she said "we" as if they would be working together. He needed to nip that in the bud right now, as well as put some distance between them for his own peace of mind. "Look, Ms. Townsend, I'm truly sorry that you and your daughter were caught up in this attack, but the FBI is investigating it, as you know, and I can't stop every few minutes to keep you informed of the progress. I don't know how long it will take, but someone from this office will be in touch with you once we have a resolution." Did her entire body just stiffen at his comment? It sure seemed that way. He stood as if to walk her out, but she didn't budge from her seat.

"I don't think you understand, Agent Springfield. I plan on participating in this investigation. I can't do a story on it because that would be a conflict of interest, but I'm definitely involved now, and I will not stop until I discover who harmed my daughter."

Chris moved toward the door, despite her show of fortitude. "I actually do understand, and I would probably feel the same if our positions were reversed. But even so, you must realize that you and your daughter are the victims. The FBI doesn't partner with victims during an open investigation. Now, like I said, someone will be in touch…" He raised his hand and gestured out the door.

She still didn't budge. "Maybe *partnering* isn't the correct word, but you do work with consultants on a regular basis."

"I wouldn't say regular…" Chris prevaricated. It was true that from time to time, they would bring in an expert to help with the specifics of a particular aspect of a case, but they certainly didn't share all of the details with any outside entity, or give anyone regular updates like she was requesting. There just weren't enough hours in the day. "But even so, working with a victim, especially one who is a member of the press, is not something we do."

She smiled. "Rules are guidelines, Agent Springfield. They are there for a reason. I understand that. But they can be broken in situations that warrant it. I have excellent research skills, and am really good at digging out the truth. Shouldn't you take advantage of the help I'm offering?" She still hadn't moved. If anything, she looked even more glued in his chair. He wondered fleetingly if he was going to have to call security to get her to leave his office. He let his hand drop.

"I'm sure you're a very good reporter," Chris hedged again. "As I said, we'll be in touch when the situation warrants it."

"You'll change your mind," Eleni said in a tone that begged him to disagree with her, however, as she said it, she jumped to her feet and stood inches away from him. She must have realized that she'd pushed him far enough, because she gave him a determined yet friendly look. "I'll see you soon." She was so near, he could smell a hint of lavender in her perfume and see tiny flecks of black in her gray eyes. She was even more beautiful up close. Her skin was smooth, and her hair looked like silk. He couldn't help himself. Unbidden, he started to raise his hand to touch her hair, but then quickly took a step back. He could feel the electricity sizzling between them as he watched her go. He hadn't felt this kind of attraction in years, if ever.

It scared him right down to his toes.

Eleni ran her tongue over her teeth as she considered her next move. She'd already been to Marino's Deli and several nearby businesses that operated by the plaza where the poisoning had occurred, but she hadn't been able to talk anyone into sharing their surveillance videos with her, or gotten any leads after she had interviewed almost a dozen people who had been working nearby during the incident.

Two days. She had already been working on this case two days and had absolutely nothing to show for it. Her boss had approved her request for leave so she could dig into what happened, and she still had some time left, but she couldn't stay away from work forever. She had to make some progress and figure out who had harmed her little girl and killed those other people before her leave ran out. As much as she hated to admit it, she needed a contact on the inside of the FBI to make any progress, and Chris Springfield was that contact, even if he didn't know it yet. Although it was obvious he was flummoxed when he was around Katie, Eleni was sure she could convince him to work with her, if she kept trying. In the meantime, she would continue to investigate on her own, regardless of the FBI's attempts to push her away.

She left the FBI building and headed south, then

stopped as she surreptitiously scanned the people on the street across from her. Even though there were six lanes of traffic that separated her from the sidewalk on the other side of the street, she still noticed a man that seemed to be following her.

Her jaw tightened. He wasn't wearing a blue jacket anymore, but the dark hair and lean build were the same. He looked quite a bit like the man she'd seen running away at the hospital. Granted, she hadn't gotten a good look at the perpetrator that had approached Katie, so this time, she tried to get a better view of the man without appearing to actually do so. His hair was graying slightly at the temples, but was mostly dark brown, a shade of russet like Katie's and her own, and he appeared to be of average height and build. He had the look of a stockbroker, professional and clean-cut, and she guessed he was in his early forties or maybe a tad younger.

She walked another block, then pretended to search for something in her purse while furtively glancing around the area.

Adrenaline pumped through her veins. Yes, he was definitely following her. When she had stopped, he had also stopped, and was now studying a window display with rapt attention.

A cold fist tightened around her heart.

Who was this man, and why was he shadowing her every move? Was he the one who had poisoned the food at the deli?

She turned and started darting around the crowded sidewalk, thankful that she was wearing casual clothes and sneakers that allowed her to run. She skidded through the front doors of a large and popular hotel, darted around the reception desk and hid herself behind a crowd of tourists in colorful clothing that were in the process of checking out. The lobby also shared space with a restaurant, and the area was crowded with several groups eating lunch. She grabbed a newspaper that someone had left behind and raised it, surreptitiously glancing around every few minutes to see if her pursuer had followed her. Fear made her heart pound against her chest, and she made a concerted effort to slow her breathing that had been coming in gasps.

He had followed her. A few minutes later, she noticed him enter the hotel through the same door she had come through, his expression grim.

She moved behind a rotund gentleman, still using the paper as a shield, as the man scanned the faces in the area. He glanced in her direction, but didn't seem to notice her. A few minutes later, she saw him exit through the other side of the hotel near the taxi stand.

She wiped her forehead with relief, but decided to stay in the lobby for several more minutes before venturing outside again, just in case the man was lurking outside, waiting for her. She was scared, but wasn't quite sure what to do about it. What could the police do? She had no proof that he was planning to harm her besides the fear that was pulsing through her veins.

One thing was for sure—she, and her daughter both, were still very much in danger.

FOUR

Two days later, Eleni jammed her hand in the closing elevator door, then pulled against it as it finally started to open again. She heaved a sigh of relief and pulled herself into the elevator, catching the eye of the only other occupant—Chris Springfield—as she straightened and adjusted her suit jacket. She hadn't seen the man who had been following her again, but had been living in virtual seclusion ever since it had happened. She was scared, but knew she couldn't hide forever. Even if investigating this case did put her life at risk, she had to do whatever she could to get the answers she needed. She met Chris's eye. "You've been avoiding me."

"No, ma'am," Chris responded as he rocked back on his heels. "I've been doing my job, which, by the way, does not include granting interviews with the press regarding ongoing investigations."

"I'm not trying to get an interview, and I'm not writing a story. My daughter and I were victims, and that guy from the hospital was following me after I left the FBI building the other day. Didn't you get my message? I tried hiding, but I just can't do it. I want to help you find out the identity of the murderer and uncover his motive just like you do. I want our lives back."

Chris shook his head. "And you've already started, haven't you? I've been fielding complaints left and right about you from the people you've been interviewing. They all want to know when you're going to stop harassing them."

"Harassing?" She shrugged. "I've been calling people, sure, trying to get answers. If people have nothing to hide, they shouldn't mind responding to a few questions so the perpetrator can be apprehended. It's their civic duty to cooperate. I promise I've been polite each and every time."

Chris took a step back. "They are supposed to work with law enforcement, not the press, and for the record, whether you're polite or not, your actions aren't helping. In fact, they're slowing me down. I don't want your help. I thought I made that clear."

Eleni raised an eyebrow. "You may not want it, but you need it." At his incredulous look, she pressed forward. "Look, I'm good at my job. I'm a respectable investigator. I've won awards for the corruption I've uncovered. Doesn't that count for something?"

"It looks great on a résumé. It does nothing to convince me I need you to work with me on this case." He pointedly took a step to the side where he could get a better view of the elevator buttons—probably so he could gauge their progress and the amount of time he had to continue talking to her. It was obvious that he didn't want to continue the conversation. She had left messages and even tried to get back into the FBI building, but he'd ignored her calls, and when she'd tried to meet with him again at his office, she'd discovered that he'd instructed the security guard at the front doors to deny her entrance. She'd had no choice but to follow him and try to meet with him in a new and creative way, but hopefully, she could thwart his attempts to exclude her here and now. With a swift move of her hand, she pushed the button to stop the elevator's progress. There was a small jolt, and the elevator quit moving and froze between floors.

He rolled his eyes. "Are you kidding me?"

"My daughter was almost killed, Agent. She's all I have, and I need answers. A man has been following me. We can't get back to our normal life and routine unless I know she's safe. I can't even have her come back home. Until the perpetrator is caught, I won't have that assurance."

Chris sighed. "I understand, but Rome wasn't built in a day. You should know that. Investigations take time, and we are doing our best to ferret out the killer. It's only been four days. You have to let us do our jobs."

She was making him uncomfortable, and she wasn't sure why. Sure, she was being a tad aggressive, but he must have dealt with other forceful victims in the past. He was an FBI agent, after all, and probably dealt with difficult people on a regular basis. She'd noticed that he'd been uncomfortable around Katie in the hospital, too, but this was something different—something that she couldn't quite identify but was about her this time, not her daughter. He wouldn't look her in the eye, and he'd backed himself into the corner of the elevator box. She wished she knew him better so she could do a better job of reading him, but how could she get to know him if he wouldn't allow any contact? Since she had this opportunity and might not get another, she observed him even closer. He had fisted his hands, and every muscle seemed tightened and tense.

Was he sweating?

She relaxed her own stance, hoping it would help him feel more at ease. She wanted answers, but she knew she'd never get them when he was wound up as tightly as an antique clock. She hoped an earnest plea would help. "Look, Agent, I'm not trying to make your life harder. What I really want to do is make it easier. Please let me help. I have to do something." She reached out and laid her hand on his sleeve. "Please."

He glanced at her hand, but didn't pull away. A moment passed, then another. Finally, he sighed and met her eye. "The names of the victims are now public record, all except your daughter, of course, because she's a minor. Five people died, and another two ladies were injured but released from the hospital after they completed an observation period. All seven need to be investigated so we can determine if there was a personal motive, or if the act was simply one of terrorism. If you want to dig into the victims' backgrounds, be my guest. Maybe you'll find something that will explain why this happened. Just don't tell anyone you're working with or for the FBI. That would be a blatant falsehood."

She smiled, squeezed his arm and removed her hand, then checked her watch. It was still early—only about nine in the morning. She could easily get a copy of the police reports that identified the victims and spend the next several hours on the internet, researching, and she had planned to go down this road anyway. In fact, she'd already started a collection of news reports regarding the incident, and as Chris had noted, some of the victims had already been identified on the local news channels. But even so, finally, it looked as if this big burly FBI agent was ready to work with her—at least a little. She pushed the button on the elevator panel that made it continue its progress up the shaft. "You won't regret it, Agent Springfield. I promise. Can we meet tonight to discuss what I find?"

He tilted his head as if surprised by her request, but finally capitulated. "Fine."

"I'll be in my office until ten or so. Care to meet me there?"

"What about your daughter?"

"She's still staying out of town with friends until this investigation is concluded. Until we identify the motive and arrest the killer, I want to make sure she's out of harm's way. Like I said, she's all I have since Charlie died. I don't want her life to be in peril while some madman is on the loose."

"Makes sense." He seemed to have a look of relief on his face. But was he relieved because Katie was safe, or because he wouldn't have to see her or be around her if they met to discuss the case? Eleni wasn't sure, but his demeanor had definitely changed once he knew the little girl wouldn't be present.

The elevator reached his floor and the doors opened. "Have a good day, Ms. Townsend."

He exited quickly, as if he was in a rush to get away from her, and she let him leave without further obstacles, then pushed the button for the elevator to take her back down to the ground floor. She still couldn't get past the idea that both she and Katie made him uncomfortable, and she had absolutely no idea why.

"I won't be able to meet with you tonight," Chris stated flatly through his phone. He'd hoped he could just leave a message for Eleni Townsend, but she had picked up after the first ring. "Something has come up." He glanced at his watch. It was around 9:00 p.m., but the stars weren't visible due to the city lighting in the downtown area. The air was crisp and clear, and despite the chill in the air, several people still walked the sidewalks, and cars and trucks still filled the streets. Chicago was like New York in some respects. It never truly slept.

"Something about the case?" she asked immediately.

"I really can't say," Chris hedged. He stood across the street at the building that housed Eleni's office, but just couldn't bring himself to go over and ride the elevator to her floor. He never really wanted to meet with her in the first place. He wasn't even sure why he'd made the trip downtown. In fact, he'd only put her to work digging up the backgrounds of the victims to keep her busy and out of his hair.

Still, Eleni was a top-notch researcher, and Chris was curious to find out if she'd discovered anything new. And she did have someone following her, which meant she could still be in danger. His protective instincts were on full alert whenever he was around her, and he was like a moth being drawn in by a flame. He just couldn't help himself, even though he knew he could never act on the attraction he was feeling.

His mind shifted through the facts they'd learned about the case. The FBI had already been doing background checks on the victims and had access to bigger and better databases than the general public, but so far, his team had gotten zilch in the motive department. Nothing seemed to stand out about any of the victims beyond Eleni and her exposé, yet they hadn't discovered any connection between Eleni's story and the poisoning. The deli itself was owned by a respectable family with a good reputation, so the attack didn't appear to have been aimed at trying to hurt the restaurant's owner either.

Usually, when a random act of terrorism occurred, there was no shortage of people or organizations rushing to take credit for the deaths, but that hadn't happened this time. In fact, not a single organization or person had claimed responsibility, which was just plain odd, and made Chris believe the poisoning hadn't been random or an act of terrorism at all.

But if the murderer had been targeting a specific person, how could the killer guarantee that the right person would be harmed in an attack like this? How did he or she know that the intended victim would eat the purple cabbage? This entire event was strange and out of left field. Of course, most folks *were* creatures of habit. If they followed a routine, they could be watched and their behavior predicted. Of all of the ideas they'd considered so far, Jerome Renfrew's did seem to be the most plausible—that one person had been the intended victim and the others were just martyred for the cause to throw off the investigation. Still, it would have to be a callous person indeed that would kill several innocent people just to get at one particular victim, especially in such a heinous way.

The FBI would keep running down any leads they uncovered. There was an answer out there somewhere. Chris and his team just had to keep looking until he found it.

He stopped his woolgathering and focused on ending the call. "Anyway, have a good evening."

"Agent Springfield, please don't hang up. I'd really like to meet with you, even if it's only for a few minutes. I've done quite a bit of research that, if nothing else, will save you a great deal of time so you don't have to spin your wheels. I've got background information on every victim from the poisoning. You'll want to hear what I've found." She paused. "If tonight won't work for you, then let's meet for lunch tomorrow. You have to eat, right?"

Chris stared at the building where Eleni was working as his mind spun. It was a normal office building, with eighteen floors and intricate carvings on the facade, built in art deco style back in the 1920s or so. Several of the windows still had lights on, despite the evening hour, but what concerned him was the smoke he suddenly saw coming out of one of the windows on the sixth floor. The sight sent off warning bells in his mind and jolted him into action.

"Ms. Townsend, what floor are you working on?" he asked, unable to keep the concern out of his voice.

"The seventh. Why?"

"Because one floor down, it looks like there's a fire in your building."

"Wait, you're downtown?" There was a pause, as if she was checking to see if anyone had reported a fire. A moment passed. "How can you tell?"

Chris realized he'd just revealed more than he'd wanted to about his location, but at this point, it just didn't matter. "Get out of the building. Now. I'm going to call the fire department." He hung up without giving her a chance to respond and immediately reported the fire, then stored his phone while glancing at the traffic, looking for the easiest and quickest place to cross the road. The corner and the crosswalk were too far away and he needed to get to Eleni now. Feelings of protectiveness and worry surged within him, and he felt powerless to stop his hands from shaking as he stepped off the curb.

What was it about Eleni that was awakening all of these long dormant feelings? One minute he was brainstorming ways to avoid seeing her, and the next, he was rushing to her rescue. He didn't want to feel anything for her or anybody else. His job was enough, and he hadn't had a meaningful relationship in quite a while. Yet here he was, running into oncoming traffic, terrified that he wouldn't be able to get to her in time.

A car nearly clipped him in the second lane he tried to cross, shaking him out of his contemplation once again as he focused on actually surviving his jaywalking attempt to get to Eleni's building. Several other drivers blew horns, and a cacophony of sounds and smells hit him as tires screeched and motors strained. The drivers were finally noticing him and the way he was waving his arms around, and thankfully the vehicles in the third lane slowed and finally stopped completely, allowing him to pass. In the fourth lane, he wasn't so lucky. There was a large bagel truck bearing down on him, and the driver was distracted and talking on a cell phone. Chris waved and yelled, trying to get the driver's attention, but it was no use. Mere seconds before impact, the driver finally saw Chris and a look of fear crossed his face as he slammed on the brakes. The truck fishtailed wildly as the metal from the grill bore down on him.

FIVE

Chris literally bounced off the hood of the bagel truck, his shoulder and left side taking the brunt of the impact. Although he'd been hit, thankfully, the truck had been slowing significantly. The impact was minimal, and he even managed to stay on his feet. He took a second to catch his breath, ignoring the pain that now radiated up his shoulder and hip. He'd been shot in the shoulder about six months ago during an assignment in Atlanta, and this new collision aggravated the old injury and made the nerves up and down his arm tingle along with the pain in his joints.

He swallowed, got his bearings and noticed that the cars in the final two lanes had stopped and were now waiting for him to cross. He waved his badge at both drivers, gave them both a grateful smile and continued his trek across the road. Moments later, he was bruised but safe and running toward the ground floor entrance, hoping that the building had a security guard or some other way to notify the workers of the danger. He said a quick prayer as he ran, thanking God for getting him across the street with his life intact.

He kept running, then slowed to glance up to see if the smoke that was coming out of the window was dissipating or getting worse. After a few more steps, he ran smack into another man with brown hair and dark gray eyes.

"Sorry," the man muttered, then put his head down and quickly moved away from Chris and continued down the street.

"No problem. It was my fault, not yours," Chris replied. He paused for a moment and watched him go, his mind filling with questions. Was that they guy he'd chased at the hospital who had tried to question Katie? He looked vaguely familiar, but he wasn't quite sure. He turned and continued on toward Eleni's building. Foe or not, his first priority had to be making sure he got Eleni safely out of the building. He pushed his way through the two sets of glass doors that led into the lobby. By the time he made his way to the security desk, he had his ID badge in his hand again and presented it front and center to the guard, who still stood with his eyebrow raised in response to Chris's dash to his desk.

"FBI. You have a fire on your sixth floor," Chris said in a tone that brooked no argument. "You need to clear this building, now."

The guard seemed in no hurry to comply. He was a sleepy grandfather type that looked aggravated rather than pleased that Chris was sharing this information.

"I don't see anything on any of the sensors. What makes you think we've got a fire?"

"I can't help what your sensors are saying. Maybe they've been disabled. What I can tell you is that you have smoke coming out of a sixth-floor window." His cell phone rang again, and he recognized Eleni's number. Was she safe and heading down to the ground floor? He answered as the elderly security guard picked up his own phone—ostensibly to call the fire department.

"I can't get out!" Eleni blurted before Chris even had a chance to greet her. "Someone has locked all the doors to the stairways. They won't open and the elevators have been shut down. People are coming down from the floors above me, too, and we're all stuck up here."

Chris felt a fist tighten around his heart. "I'm coming." He glanced quickly around the lobby and noticed a stairway to the left of the elevator bank. He turned back to the guard, still holding his phone. "The elevators aren't working, and the exit doors are locked on the seventh floor. Everyone that was working above that level is trapped. I see some stairs by the elevators. Are those the only ones?"

"No," the guard responded. "There's another set on the south side of the building that is for employees only, but those doors are kept locked, too, to keep unauthorized people from using them. The employees all have key cards, so they can get in and out. If the key cards aren't working, then something must be blocking the doors, or overriding the system."

"We can smell the smoke, and it's getting really stuffy in here," Eleni said through the phone.

Her voice had an edge to it and a tremor that made Chris's heartbeat speed up even more. "Okay. I'll start with the employee stairs. I'm heading your way now."

He stowed his phone and turned to the guard who was still on his own phone with the fire department. "...Some guy with an FBI badge...Yes, smoke..."

Chris had no patience to wait. "I need a key card to the employee stairway doors. Now."

The guard put his hand over the bottom of the phone. "I can't give you that. I'll lose my job."

"You won't have a job if the building burns to the ground. Hand over that key, now. I'll take full responsibility."

"How do I know you're even who you say you are?" the man replied. "I haven't even had a chance to run your name through the database..."

"Be my guest," Chris replied, handing the man his ID wallet. "You keep this, and I'll head up those stairs." He put his hand out. "The key. Now. I'm not asking again."

The guard finally shrugged, pulled a key card out of his pocket and put it in Chris's outstretched hand. "This will get you through any door in the building except the executive suites on the top four floors. I'll need it back."

"Fine. While I'm gone, you get as many people as you can out of this building. Everybody needs to evacuate. Now. I called the fire department, too. They should be here any minute."

Frustration ate at Chris as he grabbed the card and ran for the stairs. Did the man not believe him? Did he need to actually see or smell smoke like the people congregating on the seventh floor to shift into action? He jumped the turnstile into the employee-only area and found the south side set of stairs near the back of a hallway. With shaking hands, he touched the key card against the sensor, then grabbed the door and opened it as soon as the red light turned to green by the handle. At least the key card was working for him. He charged up the stairs, two at a time, unsure of what or who he'd find blocking the doorway on the higher floor.

By the time he'd made it to the third floor, a few of the other employees from the lower floors had already started passing him in their hurry to exit. He was glad the evacuation message was finally getting passed through the building, and he was also thankful that it was after hours and there weren't that many people still working inside. Even so, he felt like a fish swimming upstream, and several people bumped him in their hurry to exit. Was one of them the perpetrator? It was a possibility. He knew that arsonists sometimes liked to hang around and watch their work unfold. But right now, getting those doors opened so the rest of the building could evacuate was his top priority.

Once again, Chris said a quick prayer of thanks to God—this time for spurring the security guard into action. Hopefully, the building had protocols for notifying everyone when an emergency existed and they would have time to get everyone out safely, but if the doors were still locked and the elevators disabled, everyone from the seventh floor and above was currently in danger, and probably starting to panic.

He sucked in a deep breath as he hit the sixth floor and coughed as a result when the chemicals entered his lungs. Smoke had already started permeating the air in the stairwell, and he could smell the acrid scent of plastics and other synthetic materials burning. He made it to the door that led to the seventh floor and found a long metal bar braced against the door handle, keeping the door from opening if pushed from the other side. It was wedged tightly, but after several hard kicks, it finally gave way and he was able to pull the door open. A group of fifteen people or so were on the other side and surged forward as soon as the door started to open, almost knocking him over in their panic to leave the building. He regained his footing and held the door against the wall, searching the faces for Eleni. Smoke filled the musty air and whooshed into the stairway as the people rushed past him.

Chris didn't have to wait long. Eleni found him quickly and gave him a fast hug. She had her laptop bag swung over her shoulder and was wearing another blue suit jacket with navy trim that made her eyes seem an even deeper gray than they had before. He saw relief there as well as gratefulness at his presence. He was surprised by the warmth that traveled through him at her expression. And she had touched him! In fact, she'd hugged him! He had been so hurt in his last relationship that he never allowed a woman to get close—either physically or emotionally. As a result, he rarely allowed any physical contact beyond a handshake with anyone. Yet even though her hug had been fleeting, he had actually enjoyed the contact.

That thought scared him even more. He didn't want to enjoy it. This woman was inducing feelings that were most unwelcome.

"Thank God you arrived when you did! You saved us all! Folks were starting to panic in there. Apparently, the main stairwell has been blocked as well, and it was really getting harder to breathe." As if to accent the point, she coughed, grabbing his arm for support.

Chris stiffened, even though she released him as soon as the spell passed. Good grief! She'd touched him again! This time when she withdrew her hand, he suddenly felt bereft. The emotions this woman evoked made him so uncomfortable that he found himself swinging between pleasure and discomfort. He couldn't remember ever feeling so discombobulated around a woman. "We'd better get out of here and let the firefighters do their jobs," Chris said quickly to cover his uneasiness. "Do you know if everyone inside was notified?"

"Yes, the security guard issued a warning through an internal intercom system," she said. "He also told everyone to go to the employee stairwell." She raised an eyebrow. Was it her, or had she made this big bear of an FBI agent uncomfortable again? At first, she had thought it was her daughter's presence that made this man seem out of sorts, but now she wasn't so sure. He looked like a cornered wild animal. Either way, the stairwell of a burning building wasn't the place to try to analyze the issue. They both did a quick once-over of the surrounding area, and seeing no one else, she headed down the stairs with him following closely behind. The others who had previously gathered at the doorway had already rushed down the stairs ahead of them, and she was fairly certain no one else remained in the building on this floor or the ones above. Smoke made her eyes water and a host of burning smells filled the air and made her throat tighten. She hadn't seen any actual flames yet, but the fumes were permeating the entire floor as well as the stairways, and they made her sick to her stomach.

Who would want to kill and hurt so many people?

The question ate at her as she descended the stairs. She'd seen the metal pole that had been jammed under the door to keep it from opening and assumed there had also been something else blocking the stairway exit doors on the other side of the building. Even the elevators weren't working and had probably been tampered with or damaged before the fire was even discovered. Whoever had closed off the exits had obviously done so deliberately, uncaring of the consequences. Even though it wasn't the middle of the business day, the building had still held several people working after hours. If Chris hadn't come along and beaten the firefighters to the building, there might have been several people injured from the smoke, the fire or both.

Had she been the target of this latest attack? Or was this another random act of violence?

If she had been the intended victim, then why?

Questions swam through her brain as she descended the stairs. Although her latest article had garnered quite a bit of attention, her ego wasn't so inflated that she believed this event and the poisoning at the restaurant had been about her. In fact, even if she had been the target, the timing of the incidents still didn't make any sense. If someone had wanted to hurt her, it would have been before her story had been published, not a month after the fact. She was working on a few different articles right now, but none of them would have the same sort of far-reaching impact that her exposé had accomplished, and she couldn't imagine any of the subjects choosing murder as the answer to stop her current work.

But if not her, then who? She ran through the other businesses that occupied the floors above the newspaper in the building in her mind, but again, nothing stood out. There was a court innovation project, an accounting firm and the business offices for a small string of hardware stores, all of which seemed completely innocuous.

Was she simply a victim of circumstance who had been in the wrong place at the wrong time, not once but twice?

Maybe the FBI agent had some insight. She sure didn't have any. "Any idea what's going on here?" she asked Chris, turning slightly to get his attention.

He shrugged as he continued down the stairs beside her. "None. I'm hoping the fire department can help discover some clues." As if on cue, they heard the sirens in the distance and coming closer, signaling that the fire department was nearing the building.

"Do you think it's related to the restaurant poisoning?"

"Anything is possible," Chris replied, "but it seems unlikely, unless you know something I don't."

Eleni shook her head. "I can't think of a single reason why this could be about me, but even so, I sure don't like coincidences." Regardless of her words of denial, a tingle of fear crept down her spine. People were getting hurt all around her, and she needed to figure out what was going on before anyone else was killed or wounded. She thought of her daughter, who wasn't even living at home right now because Eleni didn't feel safe having her nearby.

These attacks had to stop, and stop them she would, or die trying.

SIX

"It was arson," the fire investigator confirmed. Even though the fire had occurred the day before, pungent odors still saturated the air, and Chris scrunched his nose at the acrid smell. He followed the older man through the damaged storage room on the sixth floor of the building where the remains of an old copy machines, broken furniture, and boxes of out-of-date training materials, paper and business supplies had previously been stored. The smoke had dissipated from the charred and melted contents of the room, but now what remained was a large mess of blackened heaps of refuse that still emanated an overpowering stench of burnt chemicals and plastic. He stepped over the mess, following the investigator until he stopped by a wall near one of the windows. There were burn marks on the Sheetrock, and a dark melted plastic mess near the outlet.

"Our initial impression is that the perpetrator used a timer to create a spark with a homemade device here," the investigator intoned. He pointed toward the outlet. "He used paint thinner as an accelerant, which is what caused these marks." His arm swept toward the black streaks on the wall. "There was also a large bag of Styrofoam packing peanuts placed here, near the ignition site. Once those get hot enough, they turn into a type of jelly that burns for quite a while." He motioned around the entire room. "This whole space was actually the perfect location to start a fire—an arsonist's playground. If you hadn't called in the fire when you did, it probably would have been much worse. As it is, the cleanup is going to be quite expensive, but at least no one was hurt."

Chris acknowledged the investigator's comments, but focused on the immediate problem. "You know we found the doors on the seventh floor barred, and proof that someone had tampered with the elevators. Have you had any similar crimes that match this particular arsonist?"

The investigator shook his head. "Not recently. I'll do a more thorough search once we've finished the investigation and get all of our test results, but at first impression, this is someone who took the time to do their research, but still seems rather new to the game. It very well could have been their first fire, and they were just smart enough and lucky enough to do a fairly competent job at it."

"Okay, thanks." Chris held out his hand and the investigator shook it. "I appreciate your time." He left the storage room and headed down the stairs. The elevator was working now, but he wanted the extra time to think as he walked down to the main floor.

Eleni was waiting for him at the bottom with a

group of other people who had been cordoned off behind some crime scene tape. Most of the other people were building employees waiting to be allowed back onto their particular floors to start their day. Law enforcement had refused to allow anybody but authorized personnel onto the floor where the fire had started until the investigation was completed, but had promised that some of the other floors would be opening shortly, hence the crowd of impatient workers. Chris had used his badge to get past the Chicago Police Department officer, and the same woman lifted the tape and let him pass back into the waiting throng as he approached. Eleni came up to him immediately, her eyes full of questions.

"Well? Did you learn anything?" she asked, her tone hopeful. Several people perked up and surrounded him, seeking answers, but he put his hands up and shook his head.

"Nothing I can share at this time," he replied as he continued walking toward the exit.

The others fell back, but Eleni stayed with him like glue. "I understand that you're giving them the 'no comment' line, but can't you share what you learned since we're working together?"

Chris couldn't help himself. He laughed. He didn't know if it was her expression or her words that got him, or the stress of the last few days that had been weighing heavily on him ever since he had seen poor little Katie lying in that hospital bed. "We're not working together, Ms. Townsend. I think I've made that abundantly clear."

"Eleni. You should call me Eleni," she replied, ignoring his rebuff. "Look, I did quite a bit of research yesterday into the other victims. Can we sit down and grab a coffee and just talk for a few minutes? I promise you, it won't be a waste of your time, or mine. I'd really like to show you what I found."

He did not want to sit down and talk to her. He wanted to get away from her beautiful eyes and lavender-scented skin. But unfortunately, he had more questions than answers. Would it really hurt to hear what she had discovered, if anything, if it would help with his investigation? At this point, he didn't even know if the fire and the poisoning were related in any way. If she could shed any light on what was going on, it was worth it to find out what she knew. "Okay. Coffee. Then we go our separate ways."

Her smile was instant, and lit up her entire face. "Agreed."

What a smile! She could do toothpaste commercials. He suddenly found himself wanting to see her smile more often, but then shuddered inwardly at the thought. Once again, his mind had taken him down a road that he did not want to travel.

They made their way down the street to a small open-air café, and even though the temperature was brisk, they sat at one of the outside tables and ordered coffee, croissants and blackberry jam from the waitress who met and seated them. Chris sat with his back to the building so he had a clear view of everyone coming and going—a habit he'd picked up during his younger days that he'd never quite broken. He took note of the people sitting around him as well as the people passing on the sidewalk, but once Eleni got seated and captured his attention, he had a hard time focusing on anything but her.

"So, I gather the investigator determined that the fire was deliberately set," she said as she crossed her legs under the table.

"Yes, but we pretty much knew that already since it was obvious that someone barred the doors and was trying to keep everyone from escaping the building."

"Or particularly a worker whose office was above the sixth floor," Eleni added.

"Yes." He shifted and glanced at his watch. "You mentioned you did some research you wanted to share?"

Eleni leaned forward, apparently not put off by his motion of impatience. "Direct and to the point. I like that." She pulled an iPad from her purse and opened an app that was filled with notes. "I did a thorough background history of each of the victims from the park poisoning. None of us has any connection to one another, and nobody has any veritable skeletons in the closet. Frankly, before the fire, I was starting to believe that the poisoning was just a terrorist act meant to scare innocent people, with no particular victim singled out as the target."

"But now...?" Chris stated, leaving the question hanging.

"But now, I'm starting to wonder if the fire was really a second attempt on my life. I didn't think so yesterday, but last night after I finally got home, I did a quick search of each of the victims again in relation to the building where I work. No one has any connection but me. Two of the poisoning victims don't even work downtown, and were just here sightseeing. The others work in other locations nowhere near my building."

"You're assuming the two events are linked."

Eleni raised an eyebrow. "You're not?"

Chris shrugged. "I really don't know. I *do* know I don't like coincidences either, and having two attempts on any person's life in such a short time is really unusual, and makes me start asking more questions. The fire investigator is going to compare this arsonist's MO to other fires that have taken place in Chicago, but he wasn't confident that he would find anything."

Eleni sighed. "I just can't figure out why I or my daughter would be a target."

"Can't you?" Chris asked, surprised. "What about your work?"

It was Eleni's turn to shrug. "What about it? My story broke a while ago, and I haven't had anything quite as controversial hit the news in the last month or so. If I was going to be victimized for my big financial crimes exposé, it would have happened once the story broke or even before it came out, not weeks later. Last time I checked, none of the parties arrested have even got a trial date set."

Chris paused as the waitress arrived with their coffee and food, then he buttered his croissant while thoughts swam through his mind. His research agreed with what Eleni had discovered—none of the victims knew each other, or had any apparent connections. But if Eleni's writing wasn't at the root of the attacks, then what else could it be?

He took a bite and chewed thoughtfully. "So, tell me again how often you ate at Marino's restaurant?"

Eleni took a sip of coffee and sighed with evident pleasure as the hot brew warmed her from the inside out. "Almost every day of the week, like I told you before."

Chris nodded. "And if I remember correctly, you also mentioned that you follow a similar schedule almost every day, which makes me think that you are definitely a person of habit. It would have been fairly easy to know where and when you would be eating, and even that you and Katie usually ate from the salad bar."

"But if Katie or I are really the targets, why not attack us and us alone? Why hurt so many other innocent people?"

"To make us ask these questions about the other victims and slow down our investigation, and it's working. I'm really starting to believe that hurting a group rather than an individual was intentional. Cases that don't get closed in the first few days after they happen have significantly reduced rates of ever being solved. If we can't even identify the actual target of a murder attempt, we'll probably never discover the motive, and statistics show the perpetrators will have even a higher chance of getting away with the crime."

He studied Eleni for a moment. In his eyes, she was a beautiful woman—there was no denying that.

But she was so much more than just a pretty face. She was a professional journalist who had stepped on lots of toes, and was currently digging into several different topics for other stories. But was she the intended victim all along? What if these incidents had absolutely nothing to do with her job? Who would want to hurt her? Had the fire really been a second attempt on Eleni's life? If so, why? Questions abounded in his mind as he took another bite of his croissant and washed it down with a swallow of coffee. "Okay. Tell me about you. If these attacks weren't about your work, why else would someone want to hurt you or your daughter?"

Eleni shook her head. "I really don't know. I do know my husband was killed in a car crash a year ago, and I'll never accept that it was just an accident. He was run off the road—I'm sure of it. His car ended up in the quarry in Elmhurst."

Chris frowned. "Where was he headed when the crash occurred?"

"To a property in the suburbs. He worked in real estate, and had to show a house. Actually, Katie and I were supposed to go with him, but at the last minute, Katie's stomach started hurting and I ended up staying home with her. We were planning to go out to a movie once my husband was done showing the house."

"And you think the crash was deliberate?"

"The client never even showed, so I think my husband was lured out there. Charlie was an excellent driver. He didn't drink or use drugs, he rarely sped and he wasn't exhausted that night as the police claimed.

There was no reason for his car to go into that quarry unless he was forced off the road by another car, but the vehicle was so damaged from the fall that they couldn't prove that another car was involved or not."

Chris sat up a little straighter as the dots started to line up in his mind. "So, wait, you're telling me whoever killed Charlie Townsend could very well have been trying to kill you and Katie, too? I mean, really, how was anybody to know that your daughter got sick and the two of you decided at the last minute not to come? If your husband was killed deliberately, maybe it was actually the first attempt on your life."

"I considered that," Eleni said softly. "But Charlie was killed almost a year ago. If Katie or I were actually the targets, why wait a year before trying again?"

"I don't know, but these are even more coincidences, and I don't like it." He took another bite of croissant. "Did you research to see if any of the other victims from the poisoning had any recent deaths in their families, or were involved in any other crimes?"

"I did." Eleni nodded. "They didn't. Thankfully, Katie and I were the only ones involved in any suspicious activities within the last ten years. That's as far back as I went."

Chris was quiet for a minute, thinking through everything she had told him. There was still an important piece missing. "Okay. So, tell me about this man who's been following you."

Eleni took a deep breath, then described the man the best she could and how she had lost him in the hotel lobby.

Chris put down his mug, then rubbed his hands together, warming them. "You know, I think I saw your stalker outside your building last night, right before I came up to get you out. He was out on the sidewalk."

Eleni's eyes widened. "Did you recognize him from the hospital?"

"I think so," Chris confirmed. "He had the same build and features, but I only saw him for a few seconds." He took another sip from his mug. "If you or Katie really are the target of a killer, we might not be able to discover the motive without getting a few more pieces of the puzzle. I think I'm going to need to dig into your background and see what else fits. Do you mind?" He was going to do it anyway, but if he had her cooperation, it would make it that much easier. Something wasn't right here. There were too many red flags.

Eleni shook her head. "I don't. In fact, I welcome the intrusion. I want to do whatever I need to do to get to the bottom of this so I can bring Katie home again." A cold chill suddenly went down Eleni's spine as she noticed a man standing near the corner of the street, reading a paper. He was dressed in a gray jacket and jeans, but what caught her attention was the color of his hair and his build. He looked familiar, and when he turned, her suspicions were confirmed. She leaned closer to the table and lowered her voice. "Don't look now, but the man who I saw following me is standing about thirty feet away from us on the street corner with a paper. He's trying to act nonchalant, but it's the same guy. I'm sure of it. He's wearing jeans and has on a gray White Sox jacket. Do you see him?"

Chris acknowledged her words and smiled, reacting as if nothing was out of the ordinary. Then he took another sip of his coffee as if she'd just shared the clue to a crossword puzzle. He leaned back and glanced around unhurriedly until his eyes landed on the man Eleni had described. He kept his voice low as he responded. "That's the same man I saw hanging around your building last night, right before I went in the lobby. Do you know who he is?"

Eleni shook her head, but smiled and took a bite from her croissant. She let another moment pass before continuing the conversation, hoping they were giving a realistic performance to the man who seemed to be glancing sideways over at them while pretending to read his paper. "He doesn't look familiar to me, but if he was at my building yesterday, too, maybe he's the arsonist." She couldn't keep the anger or shock from her voice. "Maybe he's the killer!"

At that exact moment, the man in the jacket looked over at her. Stormy gray eyes met her own and locked. Then the man put the paper under his arm and quickly turned and headed down the street.

Eleni slapped some cash down on the table and jumped to her feet. "He's getting away! We have to talk to him before he disappears." To her dismay, Chris Springfield was already on his feet and leaving the enclosed restaurant area, pursuing the man at the same time that he was calling in a description on his phone, and leaving her behind. Eleni hurried to follow him, wanting answers if Chris was actually able to stop the suspect and start asking him questions. Her heart pounded as the man who had been watching them noticed their pursuit and started to run, darting around the crowds. Eleni started to run as well, but wasn't a match for either man's speed, and soon lost both of them in the crowd.

What was going on? Who was following her, and why? And why would anyone want to hurt her or her family? The idea was inconceivable, and yet, it was unfolding right before her eyes and was undeniable. Someone was following her. Twice, no three times, people around her had been hurt or killed. Fear made her feel somewhat light-headed, and she paused and leaned against the brownstone of a nearby building, trying to catch her breath and calm her racing thoughts.

A few minutes later, Chris returned. He wasn't winded, but he was clearly frustrated. He ran his hand through his hair and then fisted his hands at his hips. "I lost him. The crowd was really thick three blocks down and a couple of tour buses were unloading. I have no idea if he went into a store, turned off the road or kept on going. For all I know, he jumped on one of the buses and is now headed back to a small town in rural Oklahoma." He glanced up and caught her eye. "I'm sorry. I know we need answers. Did you get a good look at him?"

"I think so. I still don't recognize him from anywhere, but he's definitely the man who was following me before." Despite her own exasperation at the man's escape, she was glad to finally have this big, confusing agent on her side. For the first time since this case had begun, she felt safe.

"Any idea why he would be following you?"

Eleni shrugged. "None. I'm sorry."

Chris tilted his head, and the look he gave her was intense. She could actually feel his pale blue eyes boring into her own. "That's one too many coincidences for me. I don't know what the motive might be, but I definitely think you're in danger."

SEVEN

Three hours. It had taken Chris over three hours to convince his boss and former partner, Tessa McIntyre, that she should allow him to protect Eleni, and now he couldn't find her. After the incident this morning at the café, and the circumstantial evidence pointing to Eleni being the target, he'd thought the decision to keep her safe would have been a slam dunk. Yet Tessa had vehemently argued against it. There wasn't enough proof Eleni was in danger. Their caseload was such that they couldn't spare him to focus on Eleni, especially without proof that her pursuer somehow fit into the bigger picture. Tessa had put up every roadblock she could muster, but Chris hadn't given in. Finally, he'd called in a favor—and promised her a favor in return—for forty-eight hours. Now he had only two days to figure out what was going on, and why Eleni and her daughter were walking targets.

But Eleni had disappeared.

Despite his misgivings and uncomfortable personal feelings, he'd wanted to keep Eleni with him after the footrace this morning down the busy Chicago street. But Eleni had wanted to check on Katie one more time, and he had been called back to the office on another matter, and they had parted ways, promising to be in touch.

Was he losing his perspective? It was a question he didn't want to examine too closely, especially since he was already struggling with whether or not he should even stay in law enforcement. Something was definitely going on with Eleni Townsend, and his instincts told him she needed his protection.

He really hoped his instincts weren't wrong.

He'd tried to find her at her office, but her boss had informed him that she'd only come by to pick up a few things, and had left over two hours ago. He'd called and texted her but hadn't gotten a response. Now he knocked on Eleni's door, shifting impatiently as he waited for her to answer. Nothing. He waited another moment or so, then checked his watch. It was around 3:00 p.m., but even though it was early afternoon, he had fully expected to find Eleni at home.

Where was she? A small seed of worry started to grow in his chest. Was she safe? Why hadn't he taken her to a hotel or safe house after trying to run down her stalker along the sidewalk?

He cupped his hands and peered in the window, trying to see inside around the curtains that covered most of the glass on the inside. Her home was a small, two-story white house with navy blue shutters and a tiny, fenced yard. Like many of the houses in the Chicago area, it was separated from the neighbor's house by a very narrow brick walkway. Although it was small, it was well-kept, like the surrounding houses, and had a neat, well-loved ambience. A dog barked down the street, but that was the only movement nearby, and he heard nothing else, either on the street or inside the house. He moved his hands against the glass, trying to get a better view. There was a small table lamp on inside, but the light was low, and he saw no movement. If he had to guess, she had left the light on and wasn't home. He tried the door, but it was locked, and he could tell the dead bolt was also engaged.

Fear for her safety started to grow even stronger within him. Had something happened? Yet nothing looked amiss or suggested anything had occurred. He left the porch and headed to the back of the house, his senses on high alert.

The backyard was empty except for a swing set and a rarely used rusty grill. He ran up the porch stairs, two at a time, and knocked loudly on the back door.

Nothing.

This time, there was no light on inside that helped him see even a stick of furniture, and he saw and heard absolutely no signs of life. Eleni simply wasn't home. According to the Department of Motor Vehicles, she didn't own a car, and by her own admission, she traveled where she needed to go by using the "L" train.

For all intents and purposes, Eleni and Katie had both disappeared.

But he was an FBI agent, with large databases at his disposal. It was hard to find a child, but adults were much easier to find in this age of technology. He went back to his car and contacted Jerome Renfrew in the basement at the FBI building, and soon had an address to check out with a promise of more if this one didn't pan out. Chris put the coordinates in his GPS and started his car. He only had a small window of time to help Eleni, and the clock was ticking.

Eleni pulled the lid off the next cardboard box of papers and other memorabilia and started sifting through the contents. There were bills mixed with old photos, worn school records and even wrinkled medical records thrown in. She had dearly loved her mother, but the lady had never been too organized, and she was still sifting through the paperwork and other belongings that had been left behind when her mother had died about four months ago. She had brought five boxes with her from the city, and planned to spend the weekend going through them in the desperate hope that something would lead her to discover who was trying to hurt her and Katie. She really was at a dead end, and didn't know where else to look. When Charlie had died, she'd done an extensive search into his background, and had found nothing suspicious. It was no wonder the police hadn't wanted to investigate his death. She hadn't been able to provide one smoking gun, or point them toward any illicit event that would have explained Charlie's death, or why someone would want to hurt him. It hadn't even occurred to her that she might have been the target all along.

A knock at her door startled her and she put her hand over her heart and took a deep breath. Who could possibly be here? She had borrowed this country home from a friend who rented it out as a vacation property in the hopes than no one, especially the mysterious man who seemed to be following her, would discover her location. Chris Springfield had promised to contact her, but she hadn't heard from him. Who could possibly be at her door? She didn't have a gun, but she did have a softball bat and several years of playing third base on her high school softball team under her belt. She moved toward the door, grabbing the bat as she went, then carefully pulled aside the curtain an inch so she could see who was on the other side of the door.

She gasped, then she quickly lowered the bat and unlocked the door and opened it. "What are you doing here?" she asked.

"Wow, thanks. Can I come in?" Chris asked, a small smile on his lips.

He looked inordinately pleased with himself, and a whisper of attraction swept over her that she didn't expect. She wasn't usually interested in such big men, or anyone involved with law enforcement because of the danger they constantly courted, but Chris had such an appealing boy-next-door grin on his face that she found herself in uncharted territory. She shook herself to make the feeling evaporate and then stepped back, making room for him to enter and talking fast to mask her befuddlement. "Sorry. I'm just surprised to see you. I didn't think anyone knew where I was."

"Your boss helped me out," Chris acknowledged. "You use a work computer and a work cell phone, and have both of them with you. They each have internal real-time tracking devices that can be turned on, as needed, even if the devices are powered off."

"I didn't even think about that." She grimaced. She leaned the bat against the wall by the door and closed and locked it once Chris was inside. "When I didn't hear from you, I figured you wouldn't be able to help me, so I just headed on out here." She turned and found her purse on an end table, then rummaged around inside until she withdrew her phone and tried to power it on. "The battery is dead." She took a moment to plug it in and noticed her missed calls and texts from him. "I'm so sorry," she said, truly meaning it. "You called and texted and I missed them all. I guess everything that has been happening has thrown me off my game. I usually don't let my phone die like that." The small house she was borrowing had an open floor plan, and she motioned him toward the living room area. "And here I was thinking I was safe and couldn't be found if I was far enough out in the boonies."

"Getting out of town was a smart idea, especially after seeing that man again today." He eyed the softball bat. "Planning on hitting a home run?"

Eleni laughed, glad that she wasn't in danger from her visitor. Despite the relief she was feeling, other emotions were also crowding in. Another whisper of attraction slid up her arms and settled in her chest, and the air felt electrified. She had to admit, he was an awfully good-looking man, especially now that his tie was loosened and his hair was mussed as if he'd just run his hands through it. Still, the attraction surprised her. Even though her husband had died a year ago, she didn't want to ever risk her heart again. It was simply too painful to lose someone she cared about, and with the death of her husband followed so closely by the death of her mom, she wanted to avoid sustaining any further hurt at all costs.

"How is Katie?" Chris asked, breaking her train of thought.

"She's doing okay. I spent some time with her like I'd planned after I left you this morning, but I ultimately decided to come up here alone. I still think she's safer if we're not together—at least until we've figured out what's going on."

Chris nodded. "Probably a smart plan." He eyed the layout of the house with a raised eyebrow, and Eleni was sure that he was assessing the safety of the building and taking in details that she would never even notice in a hundred years. His law enforcement training was deeply ingrained, and she found herself thankful for his consideration. Still, she felt awkward about his presence, especially now that she'd recognized the sparks of attraction flying between them. It was a strange turn of events, especially since she had been trying so hard to get him to work with her in the first place.

"So, I'm glad you're here. I mean, I've been chasing after you asking to help with the investigation ever since the poisoning, but what happens now?"

He suddenly quit his perusal of the small bungalow and turned his attention on her, his pale blue eyes intense. "We figure out who and why someone is trying to hurt you."

She bit her bottom lip, warmed by his scrutiny. There was caring in his eyes, and for a moment, she wondered if he was feeling the same attraction that was pulsing through her own veins. "Your boss approved?"

"It took some doing, but she finally agreed. She gave me forty-eight hours, and I intend to use every minute I can until we either find out what's going on, or eliminate you from the list as a possible target."

He made his way to a dark green velvet couch and took a seat, then motioned for her to join him. The cabin only boasted one bedroom and bath, and the rest of the place was just a large open room with the couch, a couple of striped overstuffed chairs and dark wooden shelves filled with books and country knickknacks against one wall. A small kitchen and table filled up the rest of the small room, but the cathedral ceiling made the place feel bigger than it actually was. It was tiny and simple, but simple was all that she needed. Out the back window, a crystal-blue lake with a wooden dock was visible, along with a small silver rowboat tied to the cleats, with dark red oars laying across the seats. A wooden rack was near the dock, and held two stacked sit-on-top kayaks as well as more paddles. There was a small clearing that led from the house to the water, but beyond that, a pine and oak forest filled the countryside, making the area feel secluded and private. The nearest neighbor was two miles away, or a quick paddle across the lake, but either way, she had found the solitude, and hopefully safety, she had been seeking.

"I brought your mail," Chris said, and for the first time, she noticed that he'd been carrying some envelopes. He handed them to her but she barely glanced at them before dropping them on the coffee table and seating herself in one of the overstuffed chairs, then tucking her feet up under her. She'd left her suits in Chicago and was wearing jeans and a blue oversize sweater. She figured she might as well be comfortable. She would look at the mail later. "Thanks."

"I went by your house, but didn't find you," he explained. "I was really concerned after we saw that man this morning. I'm convinced he's the same man I saw last night at the fire in your building."

Eleni sat up straighter. "I still can't figure out who he is or why he would be following me. Do you think the café or any of those other businesses along the street got a shot of him on one of their surveillance cameras?"

"No, I already checked. The guy is good. I saw his shadow a couple of places, but nobody really got a clear shot of him or his face." He pulled out his phone and leaned forward to show her some still shots of the man wearing the White Sox jacket. She recognized that it was the man they had witnessed today, but still didn't know his identity. She studied each one as he flipped through four or five pictures, but his features were fuzzy in each of the shots.

"I still don't know him. Is there enough for your facial recognition programs to identify him?"

"Nope. I tried that, too. All we could say was that he is approximately six feet tall based on the other objects in the photos." Chris pocketed his phone and leaned back. "Something else you mentioned has been bothering me." He crossed his legs. "You said that the day your husband died, you and your daughter had been planning on going with your husband in the car, but you had changed your plans at the last minute."

Eleni nodded. "That's right. Katie got a stomach-ache."

"Well, I'm thinking that his death might somehow be related to the poisoning. I can't explain why it took the killer so long to try again, but as I mentioned before, I want to dig into your past—at least for the last few years, and see if we can come up with any sort of connection. I also want to look at all of the stories you've done for the paper, and anything your husband might have been involved with. Maybe together, we can come up with some reason or motive for all of this." He shrugged. "I could be wrong, but if I am, then all I've lost is a couple of days, and I can start pursuing other avenues come Monday morning. What do you think?"

"Sounds good to me. I've been the only one investigating my husband's death since it happened, and I'd appreciate an extra set of eyes. And if the recent attacks are related at all, I want to get to the bottom of them immediately so we can stop whoever is trying to hurt us."

Chris seemed satisfied with her answer, then inclined his head toward the boxes that were filling up the kitchen table and chairs. "What's all that?"

Eleni blew out a breath. "My mother's papers. I've been working to clear up her estate. She died about four months ago from polycystic kidney disease. Since I never found anything suspicious in Charlie's history, I thought I'd start looking at other members of my family." She pointed at the boxes. "These are boxes I haven't had time to go through yet. It's a rabbit hole, and I really don't expect to find anything, but I'm running out of ideas, and thought it couldn't hurt to look."

Chris frowned. "I'm sorry to hear about your mom."

"Thanks. I tried to donate blood to help my mom at the hospital where she was being treated during her last few days, but I wasn't able to, and they didn't explain why, even though I made a big stink about it. Then a few days after her death, I received a note from the hospital, finally explaining the blood snafu. They let me know that I have a rare blood type, and I couldn't be her biological daughter." She brushed some hair away from her face. "During my entire life, I thought I was my mother's only living relative, but it turns out, I wasn't even related to her by blood. I wasn't my mom's biological daughter, after all. It was quite the shock."

"You were adopted?" Chris asked.

"Apparently." She shook her head. "My mother never told me. She never even hinted, and I never found any paperwork lying around, or anything else that made me question my family history. I mean, I realized I didn't really look like my mom, but not all kids do, you know?"

"What about your dad?"

"My mom never married. I have no idea who my father might be. Mom would never even discuss it, even though I asked her about it a lot when I was younger and realized most of my friends had fathers. Eventually, I could tell it bothered her so much that I quit asking. I figured you couldn't miss what you'd never had, so I just let it go."

"How did you feel about being adopted?"

She paused a moment, considering her response. It was an insightful question, and one she had spent a great deal of time pondering. Her respect for the FBI agent went up a notch. "I'm disappointed she didn't tell me the truth, but she was a good mom, and did an excellent job of raising me on her own. Even so, I have to admit, curiosity has gotten the best of me and I've been searching for my biological parents ever since I found out. So far, I haven't discovered any leads. I thought about doing one of those mail-in DNA test kits, but I'm not sure how accurate they are, and just haven't had time to research it yet. When I contacted the hospital to ask more questions, they were unable or unwilling to give me any more information. I'm not sure which." She frowned. "You know, the hospital did tell me something odd, though. When I kept pushing, the clerk revealed that someone else had also recently requested my blood test records, but that first request had also been denied."

Chris raised an eyebrow. "Any idea who requested them?"

"None. I can't even imagine why anyone else would care. It makes no sense to me at all. I mean, I'm almost thirty-two years old. Why would an old adoption from over thirty years ago matter to anybody?"

He stood and made his way over to the boxes, his expression thoughtful. "Have you found any answers in here?"

Eleni stood and grabbed her mail, then followed him over to the table. "None so far, but I've only had time to go through one of the boxes. This was going to be my project for the weekend. I'm really at a loss about where else to look."

She glanced down at her letters, set the junk mail aside and focused on a business-sized envelope with her typed address and no return address listed. The postmark was in Chicago. Was it another ad trying to sell her something? She opened the seal and pulled out the single sheet of paper that was inside, then peered at the strange lettering. Each letter had been cut out of a newspaper or magazine, but it was the words themselves that made her heart squeeze with fear.

i'M gOInG to KiLl yOU, aNd yOUr daUghTEr.

Eleni couldn't breathe. The words seemed to jump right off the page and strangle her. She stumbled, then fell into the nearby seat and tried to regain her equilibrium. Chris grabbed the letter and scanned the page, then put both the letter and the envelope on the table, squatted down in front of her and took her hands firmly in his own.

"Look at me," he said, waiting a moment for her to meet his eyes before he continued. His expression was resolute and firm, and she saw determination in those blue depths and a quiet strength that she rarely encountered. He squeezed her hands, which had suddenly grown cold and painfully stiff. When he spoke, his tone was fierce. "No one is going to hurt you, Eleni Townsend, or Katie. I'm going to make sure of it. If someone even tries, they'll have to go through me first."

EIGHT

Chris was completely nuts.

Had he just promised to protect this woman and her child, regardless of the consequences? The words had left his mouth before he could stop them, and he was still totally dismayed at the attraction and protective feelings he was developing toward Eleni. He wasn't looking for a relationship. And even if he were, getting involved with a victim from a case was strictly taboo.

And what about Katie? He didn't want to be around children. In fact, every child reminded him of the dead little girl he'd lost during his last case, and caused an ache in his heart that was nearly debilitating. Good grief! He wasn't even sure he would still be an FBI agent next week. He was still going back and forth about whether or not he could even do this job anymore. He gritted his teeth, strangely nervous about his vow, yet for some reason he couldn't or didn't want to identify, he couldn't bring himself to immediately take back the words.

Eleni squeezed his hands, then led him back over

to the couch and ended up sitting beside him. Her hands were warm again, and he found himself enjoying her closeness. Suddenly, despite her fear that the letter had invoked, she was now the stronger one, and he could tell that there was no way she was going to let him off the hook without an explanation. She turned and their eyes locked. "I heard what you said, and I truly appreciate your attitude, but I also see this look on your face that is somewhere between terrified and horrified. Do you want to explain?"

He didn't. He hadn't even shared his feelings with Tessa, who was like a big sister to him. There was something about Eleni that drew him closer, despite his misgivings and concerns. He couldn't explain it. He didn't even want to analyze it. All he knew was that he felt at ease with her, as if he could talk to her and she would listen without judging him. He hadn't felt that camaraderie and compatibility with anyone else in a really long time. The sentiments made no sense to him, and scared him on a totally new level. He'd only known Eleni for a few days, and had only spent a small amount of time with her. How could he feel this way about someone that was virtually a stranger? Still, he couldn't deny the peace he felt just by being around her. She exuded strength and joy without even trying.

He backpedaled anyway. He wasn't ready for these feelings. He didn't want to even admit they existed. It was better for both of them if he just packed them away and locked them up, deep in his heart. He was a mess inside. That last case had thrown him for such a loop, it was no wonder he didn't know if he was coming or going. It wasn't fair to offer anyone more than he could give, and once they solved this case, they would each go their separate ways. She would return to her life and her daughter, and he would return to… return to what? The career that he wasn't even sure he wanted anymore? Turmoil twisted inside of him.

"I shouldn't have said that," he finally acknowledged. He scooted farther away from her, and she noticed, but didn't comment. "During my last case, a little girl was kidnapped and murdered. I've had bad outcomes before, but nothing like that. Now I'm not even sure if I want to stay in law enforcement. Maybe I'm not cut out for this type of work. I don't know." He ran his hands through his hair in exasperation. "Either way, I shouldn't be making any promises right now. Especially those I can't keep." He grimaced. He couldn't leave it like that either, steeped in uncertainty. "Look, I can tell you that for the next two days, I'm going to do everything I can to figure this out. If you have been targeted, and it certainly looks like you have, then we need to stop the perpetrator before he tries to hurt you again…or hurts anybody else."

She didn't say anything for a moment or two. Then she smiled at him. "Are you hungry?"

He blinked. Had she just drastically changed the subject? He tilted his head, trying to read her. "Yes, I guess. I kind of skipped lunch when I was running around Chicago, looking at store surveillance tapes and trying to find you." He glanced around the cabin. "Do you have anything here to fix? This place isn't exactly on the Magnificent Mile." In fact, they were out in the boonies, at least an hour away from Chicago, and he hadn't passed any stores or restaurants during the last thirty minutes or so of his trip out to find her, so he doubted there was much to choose from if they needed to find a place to eat.

"Of course. I was planning on staying here for the weekend, so I brought food with me, but if you're wanting a Michelin star meal, you'll be sadly disappointed. I was thinking of just whipping up some pancakes. Can you handle that?"

"Got any bacon?"

She put up her hands and tilted her head with an expression of disbelief. "Of course!"

"Deal." He stood. "First things first. I need a plastic storage bag to put that letter in. As soon as I get back to town, I'll take it to the lab to have them check for fingerprints, although I doubt there will be any. If the sender was careful enough to avoid writing anything so we couldn't identify the handwriting, he or she was probably careful enough to wear gloves."

"Agreed." She stood and moved over to the kitchen, then rummaged around in the cabinet until she came back with a zippered storage bag for the letter. A few minutes later, she was stirring the pancake batter in a ceramic bowl, and he had secured the letter and gotten it ready for the lab. "You can fry up the bacon while I get these pancakes going. It's in the fridge, and the pan is under the sink."

He followed her directions, and soon had the bacon sizzling on the stove. The small cabin was suddenly permeated with wonderful cooking smells, and he took a deep breath, letting the comfort food soothe him. He flipped a couple of pieces over, watching her surreptitiously out of the corner of his eye as she poured batter on a small griddle. "So, you let me off the hook pretty easily a few minutes ago."

She glanced in his direction, but kept her focus on the pancakes. "Yes, I did. I'm really glad you told me about that case, and I'm so sorry you had such a horrible outcome. What you told me actually explains a lot of questions I've been having the last few days. Since I first met you, I've gotten the impression that Katie and I make you feel uncomfortable. Now I understand why. I didn't want to make you feel worse by asking you a lot of questions when you clearly needed some space."

"I appreciate that." He moved the bacon around in the pan some more, still uncomfortable and not wanting to look her in the eye. "But as long as I'm baring my soul, I should probably admit that I'm attracted to you, and it scares me to death."

She smiled, but again kept her focus on the pancakes. She must have sensed intuitively that he was still struggling, and he appreciated the fact that she was giving him time to work through his thoughts.

"Why are you scared?" she asked gently.

"Because my last relationship didn't end well, and my entire future is up in the air at this point. That last case has me reconsidering my entire future." He shrugged. "I'm not any grand prize anyway."

She laughed. She actually laughed at him! He

wasn't sure how he felt about that. He wasn't used to being laughed at, and actually hadn't laughed himself in quite a long time. He frowned, thinking back over his words. "Is what I said really that funny?"

She finished pulling the pancakes off the griddle and turned off the power, then turned to face him, her hands on her hips. "Are you kidding? Good grief, Agent Springfield! You're one of the most attractive men I've ever met. I know at least a dozen women who would love to settle down with you if you gave them even the slightest indication that you were interested." She smiled, even though he knew he had a look of abject disbelief on his face. What she was saying couldn't be true. He was too big, too awkward, to attract anyone of Eleni's caliber. He knew that. Maybe she was just being kind. She reached out and gently touched his face as she continued, "You're a strong and professional man with a wonderful future in front of you. I realize you're going through a rough patch right now, but you'll work through it, and come out better on the other side, whether you stay with law enforcement or not. That's just the type of person you are. It's as plain as the nose on your face."

She was touching him again. But even if she wasn't, he would still be frozen in place by her words. Attractive? Him? He'd always thought of himself as an oversize grizzly bear, graceless and shy, especially around women. And she'd only known him for a short time. How could she make such bold statements?

"You're burning the bacon."

"Oh!" He quickly stepped back to move the pan

off the burner and turned the power off, then used the tongs to take the bacon out and lay it flat on a plate covered with paper towels to drain. "Sorry." He'd never met someone like Eleni, who was so transparent, so honest. He certainly didn't have to wonder what she was thinking. He liked that. Her next words even further convinced him.

"Look, I feel the attraction between us, too. I'd be lying if I said I didn't. But I've lost so much in the last year, that it scares me to even consider going down that path." She looked over at him again, but this time her gaze lingered. "But I hope you understand, my hesitance has absolutely nothing to do with you. Does that make any sense? I know I probably seem like this tough, aggressive reporter that's not scared of anything. But I'm actually afraid to fall in love again. I can handle a lot, but I don't think I could manage losing someone else I care about." She moved the boxes away from the table, then grabbed the plate of pancakes and carried them to the table. "I guess that's why I'm so driven to protect Katie. Losing her would destroy me."

Chris brought the bacon over as well. Once again, he was surprised by her words and her plain speaking. "You're tougher than you think. And what does the Bible say? 'I can do all things through Christ.'"

She raised an eyebrow. "So, you're a Christian?"

He smiled. "I am. You?"

"Me, too," she said, as she handed him an empty plate and some silverware. "Maybe we should both take your advice, and let God take care of the hard stuff. I pray and try to give things to Him, and then a few minutes later, I end up grabbing the stress and worry right back. I'm not very good at 'letting go and letting God.'"

"I do the same thing," Chris replied. "I find myself struggling the most when I forget to include God in the equation."

It was her turn to smile. She brought over two glasses of ice water, some syrup and butter, and then sat and motioned for him to take the other chair. "So now that we've both acknowledged our feelings, where do we go from here?"

He sat, then reached out his hand so they could pray before eating. "Well, I can always use another friend, and if we're going to be working together to solve this mess, that seems like a pretty good place to start. Why don't we just focus on that?"

"Agreed." Eleni nodded and took his hand. "Let's pray and eat, friend!"

Chris blessed the food and the two dug in, neither one shy about filling their plates. Eleni had done her best to put the big FBI agent at ease, and it seemed to be working. She could tell he was still struggling, but the issues that were bothering him didn't have a quick fix. She was honored, though, that he had given her a glimpse into his pain. He'd also seemed truly shocked that she found him so attractive, and she was glad that her words had helped heal even a little of the emotional scars he carried. It was obvious that neither one of them were in a place to act on the attraction that existed between them. But the man was hurting, and if she could do anything at all to help him, she wanted to do that. She reached for another slice of the crispy bacon and smiled. It was still edible. A little overdone on the edges, but edible.

The awkwardness and electricity that had been sizzling between them lessened, and had been replaced by a comfortable camaraderie. It was good to know he was a Christian. That meant a great deal to her, and she was glad she'd shared her own relationship fears with someone who had similar beliefs. It gave their friendship a good foundation that they could both build upon.

"So tell me about your husband, Charlie Townsend," Chris asked between bites.

Eleni shrugged. "Sure. What would you like to know?"

"Anything. Everything. I'm trying to find any link at all between your family and the murders. Even the smallest detail might help."

"Well, we met in college, at Loyola University downtown, to be specific. I was a scholarship kid focused on journalism, and his major was business. We graduated the same year, and then he went on to get his MBA while I started working at a small publishing house. After Charlie got his master's, he got a job in real estate, and stayed at the same company until his death. He handled residential properties, never commercial. He never had any complaints and wasn't involved in any shady dealing or lawsuits." She took a sip of water. "We're pretty ordinary people,

Agent. That's another reason why this whole thing is so strange. I can't imagine why anyone would want to hurt any one of us."

Chris sat back. "The only thing that strikes me as a possibility is your work on your last exposé. But as you said, if they wanted revenge or even to stop your work, the timing of these recent attacks just doesn't make sense, and then Charlie's death wouldn't be involved either." He pushed a piece of pancake around in a puddle of the syrup on his plate. "You know, sometimes, we don't know what we don't know. I wonder if you, Charlie and Katie saw a crime or something else that looked ordinary enough at the time, but the perpetrator doesn't want you to make any connections. They could be moving proactively to take you out of the mix so your testimony could never come back to hurt them."

Eleni grabbed the last piece of bacon and gave him a sheepish grin. He smiled and motioned for her to keep it, so she took a bite, chewing thoughtfully. "It's possible, I guess. But I really don't remember anything odd or out of place happening in the last few weeks, or even before Charlie died."

Chris's cell phone rang, and he stood and took the call, taking his empty plate over to the sink as he spoke to the caller. Eleni could tell it was a business call, so she busied herself with clearing the rest of the table and starting the dishes. It didn't take her long to finish, and she went to the pantry and pulled out two empty brown paper bags, then sat down at the table again and pulled out a handful of papers from the top of the closest of her mother's boxes. She sorted through them, putting the papers that needed shredding in one bag and the items she wanted to keep or look at a second time in the other. This first handful of paperwork was old phone and electric bills, and she was quick to dump those in the recycle bag. She had no idea why her mother would have saved these in the first place, but she couldn't think of a use for them, and the accounts had been closed upon her mother's death, so getting rid of them all seemed like the smart move.

A few minutes later, Chris returned to the kitchen area, stowed his phone and sat back down. "Good news! Because of the chemical makeup of the cyanide that was used to poison everyone at the restaurant, our lab was able to track down the manufacturer, who just provided us with their sales receipts. We have a suspect. His name is Henry Jackson, and he started working at the restaurant about two months ago as a dishwasher. Apparently, he was using a fake name and social security number at Marino's, which is why his true identity didn't pop up in our initial inquiry." He smiled inwardly. "I owe our tech guy a gift card for Chick-fil-A. He's the one that noticed the discrepancies and discovered the problem."

"Chick-fil-A?" Eleni questioned.

"Yep, he'd eat there every day if he could. I wouldn't be surprised if he moonlights there on the weekends."

Eleni laughed. "Probably the best money you'll ever spend, right?"

Chris smiled in return. "You bet." He stood. "I'm

going to head into town and join in the raid. Are you game?" He glanced at his watch. "If we leave now, we'll miss the arrest, but we can walk through the perpetrator's apartment and see if you notice anything that might tie him into the case."

He was actually going to let her come along! She jumped to her feet. "You bet," she said, repeating his earlier words.

He grabbed the plastic bag that had the letter inside. "I also want to get this to the lab ASAP. If it had Jackson's fingerprints, we'll be halfway home with this case."

Eleni couldn't believe it. Chris Springfield was not only going to share information with her, he was also going to let her accompany him back to Chicago and walk through the perpetrator's apartment. "Thrilled" didn't begin to describe her excitement. Finally, it looked as if they might actually have a lead that could help them figure out this mess. Then she could bring her daughter home, and life could return to normal once more.

NINE

Something was wrong.

The area around the house had been cordoned off with crime scene tape, which was normal. Several officers were standing around talking in hushed tones, though, and the air felt thick and oppressive. Chris did a fast parking job, and then he and Eleni got out of the government-issued sedan and headed over to where the nearest Chicago PD officer was standing just inside the tape. Chris flashed his badge, then motioned for Eleni to follow him.

"She's with me," he noted to the cop, who nodded and raised the tape so the two of them could enter the crime scene area. The officer used his radio to announce their arrival to the agent in charge of the scene, just as the coroner's vehicle arrived and parked behind them.

"I was afraid of that," Chris muttered in a low tone. He tried to hide the distress he was feeling, but didn't succeed.

"What?"

"With the coroner here, it means either the perp is dead, or one of the agents got killed during the arrest."

She squeezed his arm. "Let's go find out before we start guessing."

"Agreed." They took the porch steps up to the front door and put on the protective booties and rubber gloves they were handed by an officer at the entry-way. Steve Taylor, the agent in charge of the FBI's local special weapons and tactical team, met them with a nod. Steve was another large man, similar in build to his own, but with gray hair at his temples and lines of experience etched in his face. If Chris had to guess, he'd figure Steve was a good ten years older than his own thirty-three years, but the man was in amazing shape, and was sharp as a needle with intelligent brown eyes that missed absolutely nothing. He was dressed in combat gear as they always did when entering an unknown situation. Chris didn't socialize with Steve, but he had worked with him a time or two in the past. He shook hands, introduced Eleni as a consultant and put his hands on his hips. "So, what have we got?"

"When we entered, we found the perp dead on the kitchen floor. He'd been shot twice in the chest. I'm guessing it was a .45, but I'll let the coroner confirm that. We've got one slug we've dug out of the wall. We also found something else you'll want to see." He motioned for both of them to follow him, and took them down the stairs into the basement. In the middle of the room, there was a large worktable covered with old screws, nails, bottles, tin cans, and bits of machines and metal components. A sour smell permeated his senses, and he wrinkled his nose. The stench was a mixture of chemicals, mold and stale body odor. Apparently, their perp had spent a lot of time down in his basement, but hadn't worried about cleanliness.

"What's all this?" Chris asked.

"Well, the guy won't win any points for neatness, but we did find this interesting." He pulled a pen from his pocket and pointed at a small brown glass bottle. It was clearly marked "cyanide" and had the name of the manufacturer on the label as well.

"Does it match up with our restaurant cyanide?"

"It's the identical brand, and the size and color of the jar corresponds to the order we found. We'll have to confirm that the chemical compounds are the same with our lab, but it looks like we've found our killer. Now we've just got to figure out who murdered him and why."

A chill went down Chris's spine and a touch of nausea churned his stomach. He'd never get used to the death that he encountered through his job. Maybe that was a good thing. When death became so common that he ignored how it made him feel, then it was definitely time to find a new line of work.

"We'll take a look around, then head back upstairs," Chris announced. Steve nodded, then turned and left them in the basement alone.

"I can't believe a person can order cyanide and have it shipped through the mail like a pair of socks or a bottle of vitamins," Eleni commented as she studied the contents of the shelves.

"You'd be surprised what you can order off the internet," Chris replied. "Even controlled substances are getting easier to get. Unfortunately, some people are more interested in making a profit than they are ensuring public safety, and international markets don't have the same restrictions we have here in the states."

"Maybe I'll make that the subject of my next article," Eleni mused. "It sounds like the issue needs to be brought to light."

"Now, that's a great idea," Chris agreed with a nod. "I look forward to reading that."

They spent several minutes perusing the basement, looking for any other clues that might tie the shooting victim to the poisoning and the other recent crimes. At one point, Eleni pointed to a dead rat in the corner that had obviously been there quite some time. "Have you ever seen such a mess?"

"Unfortunately, yes. Many of the people we arrest are not too worried about cleanliness."

"The dirt is one thing," Eleni said, "but this smell! It's horrific. It makes me want to open a window or two. I don't know how anyone could actually work down here for any length of time."

Chris smiled. Few civilians realized everything people in law enforcement had to deal with on a regular basis. "Agreed, but thankfully, we'll only be down here a few minutes. Keep looking and let me know if you see anything out of the ordinary or strange to you."

"I'm not sure what I'm looking for. Do you know?"

"No idea," Chris stated as he studied the items on the table, "but since we're still hunting for our perp's motive, just try to keep an open mind."

"Okay."

They both moved slowly around the basement, taking in the items stored haphazardly around the room. The shelves were filled with old paint cans and fertilizer packs, and the pegboard on the wall was covered with hooks of various sizes and held several garden implements and tools, which Chris found ironic since the man's yard was in total disrepair. They had probably belonged to a previous owner, and had just never been removed. He looked toward the corner underneath the stairs. Even the rust-covered washer and dryer looked as if they had both seen better days. Water stains and chemical burns surrounded the wall and floor near a small utility sink.

They spent a few more minutes studying the area, and Chris even snapped some photos with his phone before they went back upstairs. They headed to the kitchen next, where there was a man in jeans and a green T-shirt lying with his back on the ground. Two bloodstains marred his chest where the bullets had entered his body and ended his life. His eyes were still open, and his face had a frozen expression that still showed surprise. The victim was Caucasian with brown hair, and his body had taken on a discolored, bloodless hue. Chris guessed he was in his thirties, but looked older, probably because of methamphetamine use. He had the poor skin and teeth that pointed to the drug habit, but the autopsy would confirm his hypothesis.

"Recognize him?" Chris asked.

Eleni moved so she could get a better look. "No, sorry."

Her voice was softer than Chris expected, and he glanced at her direction. Was she turning a little green? Blood was spattered all over the floor behind the body, and had also formed a pool on the floor around his back. It wasn't a pretty sight, and the smell in this room was worse than the smell in the basement. Chris had seen his share of horrific scenes, but he was fairly certain Eleni hadn't. What had he been thinking, bringing her to a crime scene? His first instincts had been correct. He should never have let her get involved in the investigation.

"Let's get out of here," he said, gesturing toward the door they had come in through.

"Wait." Eleni wanted nothing more than to make a quick exit, but something odd had just caught her eye. There was a recycling container by the refrigerator, and inside, she saw several old newspapers and magazines amongst the beer cans. What interested her, though, were the clippings that were also in the box and spilling out onto the floor. She stepped carefully around the body and reached in for one of the papers. There were holes where certain letters had been cut out. "I wonder if these missing letters match the letters in that horrible note I got in the mail." She held up the paper and looked at Chris through the holes. "There can't be too many people cutting out letters and sending hateful notes through the mail."

He smiled. "Good find!" He motioned to one of the officers that was standing nearby and asked for an evidence bag. He put the newspaper inside along with one of the magazines that also had letters cut from the pages and then marked the bag. "I wish I could tell you that you were safe, now that we know that the killer is dead, but he sure didn't die from natural causes. Now we have even more questions."

"And it means this might be bigger than we originally thought," Eleni added, following him out. Did the man's death mean the criminals who had planned the poisoning had a falling-out, or was there another reason for his murder? And what, if anything, did the man that had been following her have to do with this? The features of the man who'd been wearing the White Sox jacket didn't match the man who lay dead on the kitchen floor. She pushed the thoughts aside as her stomach twisted, and she ran out the front door, stopping at the bottom of the steps and taking a deep breath, trying to regain her equilibrium and enjoy the fresh air that filled her lungs. The smells she'd encountered in the basement were nothing compared to the smell of death surrounding the body in the kitchen. It had obviously been there a couple of days, and the scent still seemed to coat her nostrils. She was glad Chris had allowed her to come, but it would be a while before she could forget the sights and smells she'd just encountered. She had asked to be included—begged even. She could hardly complain now that she'd gotten what she'd asked for. Still, she really hoped she didn't lose her pancakes here on the overgrown lawn of the man who had tried to kill her and her precious daughter.

"You okay?" Chris asked, worry in his tone.

"I will be," she responded. "I'm not used to being around death." She eyed him speculatively. "I don't know how you do it."

"It's the worst part of the job," he agreed. "Well, almost the worst."

"What could be worse than that?"

He stopped walking and the expression on his face was pure pain and sorrow. She was immediately sorry she'd asked. She didn't want to think about what was worse, and she could tell her question had brought up memories that were best left alone. He had obviously witnessed much worse, and probably on more than one occasion. "Never mind," she murmured. "What are the best parts?" she asked, hoping to turn the conversation into a positive tone.

Chris looked startled by her question. "There aren't many."

Eleni frowned. "Really? I would think that helping people get justice ranked pretty high up on the list. When someone's life has been destroyed, your team comes in and helps put the pieces back together again. I would think that would be rewarding, and I know you've had a successful career." She shrugged, unrepentantly, when he raised an eyebrow. "I looked you up." He was silent for a moment, and she gave him a nudge. "Don't worry. I'm sure most of your career is not open to the public eye. But you have been a part of some cases that had wonderful conclusions. Like that money laundering case down in Atlanta. I came across that case when I was doing research for my big exposé. You stopped Bryce Cameron, who was operating a major international scheme. That case alone was quite the accomplishment."

"His real name was Shawn Parker, and yes, he'll be in prison for the rest of his natural life. I was part of the team that worked that case, but I got taken out early. I was shot in the shoulder by a guy trying to kill our star witness."

"That wasn't in the reports I read," she said softly. "Are you okay now?"

"My wound healed. I had to do some physical therapy before coming back full-time, but I'm pretty much back to normal now." He rotated the arm and shoulder that must have been affected. Eleni realized he probably didn't even know he was making the subconscious motion as he spoke about his injury. "You wouldn't have seen a report. They don't usually release the names of the agents that are injured to the public."

"Well, I'm really glad you healed up so well. I don't know if you get thanked often enough for the sacrifices you make, but thank you."

"Sacrifices?" He seemed genuinely puzzled.

"Of course!" Eleni replied adamantly. "I have always highly respected those who choose law enforcement for a career, even if I struggle to get along with them, like I did with the officers who investigated Charlie's death. You put yourself in harm's way each and every day that you're on the job. It takes a special kind of person to do that."

"I'm no hero," he said softly, real pain in his voice. She could see a muscle tighten in his jaw. Was he that unhappy with his current profession? What had happened to hurt him so?

"I've had some successes, sure," he responded before she had a chance to ask anything further. "But I've had more failures than successes lately. I guess it's made me see things with a more cynical eye. I'd be lying if I said I had it all figured out." He ran his tongue over his teeth. "You know, I don't really want to talk about this."

Eleni put up her hands in a sign of mock surrender. She didn't want to push him into a conversation that he clearly didn't want to have. "Fine by me. I'm really sorry if I touched a sore spot."

"It's okay," he responded. "It's only sore because I'm still working through it." He ran his hands through his hair. He looked up and caught her eye, and she saw a despair and frustration she hadn't expected. "Actually, maybe I do need to talk about it."

Eleni gave him a smile that she hoped showed kindness and understanding. She touched the side of her head. "Look. I have two ears, no waiting." They were still in front of the suspect's house, and a stream of people, including the coroner and the coroner's assistant, were coming and going from the residence. This was not the place to continue talking, especially with so many people milling around. They had been keeping their voices down, but she still didn't want to have anything either of them said to be overheard or misinterpreted. He was amongst his own here, but privacy was still warranted. She nodded toward the sidewalk across the street beyond the crime scene tape. "Let's take a walk, okay? You don't have to say a word unless you want to, but I'd like to stretch my legs. The rest is totally up to you."

TEN

Chris felt his muscles clench. What was he doing? Had he just agreed to share parts of his life story—the most sensitive and damaging parts—with a virtual stranger who was a reporter to boot?

Was he crazy?

Maybe he was. Because even though he hadn't known Eleni very long, he already felt a closeness to her that he couldn't quite explain. He felt at ease around her, plain and simple, and he hadn't felt that way around anyone, even his old partner, Tessa, for a very long time. Eleni wasn't critical. She didn't jump to conclusions. He liked that. "Walking sounds good."

They left the crime scene area and started down the sidewalk at a comfortable pace. He didn't say anything for quite a while, and just enjoyed the camaraderie. Finally, he had to ask, just to be sure, "So, you're a reporter, and…"

"I would never write about anything you tell me in confidence, Chris. You have my word. And I don't make promises lightly."

Was that the first time she had called him by his

first name instead of "agent"? He liked the way his name sounded on her lips. He also believed her. Although she had the reputation of being aggressive when going after a story, he'd never heard anyone accuse her of being unethical. He believed her vow, and realized he trusted her to do what she said. That was a revelation in itself for him. He hadn't relied on anyone who wasn't a colleague or fellow FBI agent in quite some time.

But believing she would keep her word was one thing. Trusting her with his heart was something else entirely, and something he wasn't ready to do. They had agreed to be friends and nothing more, despite the mutual attraction that simmered between them. That decision suddenly seemed like one of the wisest ones he'd made in quite a while. Friends could talk without expecting more. Friends could listen without judging. And right now, he desperately needed a friend.

"I've always thought working for the FBI was a chance to make a difference and help people, like you suggested, but that money laundering case I worked in Atlanta was one of the only positive outcomes I've had in a long time." He was glad they were walking. It was easier to talk to her when he wasn't looking directly in her eyes. "I think you already know that right now I work with a special team at the FBI that focuses on investigating violent homicides and terrorism cases. But after college, I started out as a sniper with the Army Rangers, and I did several tours in the Middle East, or the sandbox, as we called it. I only moved over to the FBI about five years ago."

"How did you feel about being a sniper?" Eleni asked, true interest apparent in her voice.

"I didn't go into the army expecting that job, but I'm pretty good at shooting, and that's where I ended up."

She raised an eyebrow. "That's not what I asked."

"I realize that," he said softly, still not meeting her eye.

She took the hint and didn't push as they made it to the end of the block, crossed the street and started up the next one. "So what attracted you to the FBI?"

"It was a mixture of public safety and intelligence, which I found intriguing."

"And you find it less intriguing now?"

"It started out fine, but my last few cases have been truly horrific. My last case was the worst. I already told you that we had this missing little girl who was just a little bit older than Katie. She was kidnapped, and the parents decided to do the money drop on their own without FBI involvement." He could hear his voice breaking and hoped he could keep it together. "The kidnappers took the money, but killed the child anyway." He was silent for several moments, then continued, "I was the one that found the body." His tone was nearly a whisper. "It was the worst thing I've ever seen. I still have nightmares about it."

Eleni didn't say anything, but she put her hand in his, intertwined their fingers and squeezed gently. It was as if she was offering him a lifeline, and he took it, enjoying the warmth and support she was offering.

"I thought Katie made you a bit nervous. Now that makes perfect sense."

"I hate to admit it, but she does. She's a sweet kid, but every child makes me nervous now. And unfortunately for me, Katie looks a little like the victim."

Eleni was quiet for a moment, then asked, "Would it have made a difference if the parents had cooperated?"

"Maybe. I'd like to think so. But there are really no guarantees. And I understand where they were coming from. They were terrified, and doing what they thought they needed to do to get their daughter back. I really can't blame them for their actions. I mean, who's to say I wouldn't have done the exact same thing if our positions were reversed?" He clenched his jaw. "There are some really bad people in this world, and they do horrible things, even when good people try to stop them."

"Were you able to catch the kidnappers?"

"We got one of them, but all the evidence pointed to a pair, and the other was never identified. He's still out there, probably enjoying the high life with his ill-gotten gains. It makes me sick just to think about it." He sighed. "I guess the bottom line is that I'm just tired. Tired of the villain winning. Tired of seeing firsthand what an evil mind can do to the innocent people that just happen to be in the wrong place at the wrong time."

"Do you listen to Christian music?"

Chris raised an eyebrow. He was a bit surprised by the change in subject, but took it in stride. "Sometimes."

"Well, I personally find music very therapeutic,

and Christian music can be amazingly uplifting. There's a song by Jordan St. Cyr called 'Weary Traveler' that I heard on the radio this morning. Some of the lyrics say, 'you were never meant to walk this road alone.' It was a great reminder that I need to make sure that I'm including God in my life—especially during the difficult times." She squeezed his hand gently. "It sounds like you might be considering a career change. Have you talked to God about His plans for your life, and where He wants you to be?"

Chris considered how to answer that, and they went a full block in silence. "Yes, and no. I mean, I've prayed about it, but…"

"But?"

He sighed. "But I haven't really given the situation over to God completely. And I haven't made any hard and fast decisions yet. I'm just unhappy where I'm at, and I'm not sure what to do about it. I know He's up there in heaven just looking down, shaking His head at me and wondering if I'll ever get it right…"

Eleni laughed. "I doubt that! But finding God's will for your life can be tough if you're not paying close attention. As you are searching for God's will for you, it's important to be sure you are fully open to whatever God wants. He'll lead you in the right direction if you're open to options, but if you make a decision without consulting Him and then just ask Him to rubber-stamp your choice, you may be disappointed with the outcome." She squeezed his hand. "Do you have something else in mind that you'd rather be doing?"

Chris shook his head. "I haven't really even started

exploring other options. I just know I'm not happy where I am."

Eleni nodded. "Well, it's possible that God wants to move you into a different area, or He might want you to stay where you are, and grow where you're planted. You just don't want to mistake your own thoughts and desires for God's voice. You have to be open to letting God guide you in any direction, even if that direction stretches you in ways that make you uncomfortable. When your desire to follow God's plan for your life outweighs your own desire for a certain outcome, well, that's when you're truly ready to hear from God." She smiled at him. "In any case, I think the answer you're looking for is to stop trying to figure this all out on your own. God has a plan for your life. You know that verse in the Old Testament—Jeremiah 29:11? It says, *For I know the thoughts that I think toward you, saith the Lord, thoughts of peace, and not of evil, to give you an expected end.* Only God knows if you're supposed to stay in your current profession, transfer or find something new. The key is to pray to God, and let *Him* direct your steps, not your frustration or disillusionment. If you truly seek His will, you'll have your answer." She squeezed his hand again. "Does that make any sense at all?"

He walked in silence for several steps, mulling over her answer. She had certainly given him a lot to think about. "It does. And if I make the decision without including God in the process, I'm apt to go down the wrong path."

"Exactly," Eleni agreed.

Chris stopped and looked around. They had walked several blocks, and the forty-eight-hour time frame that Tessa had allowed was quickly slipping away. Just walking and talking had been therapeutic, though, and Eleni's insightful comments had been spot-on. He couldn't regret taking a few minutes out to talk. "We need to get back. My boss only gave me two days to find answers, and the clock is ticking."

They turned and headed back toward the car, just as Chris's phone began to ring. Chris released Eleni's hand and took the call, his mind instantly back on FBI business.

Eleni tried not to eavesdrop, and instead focused on the advice she had just given Chris. There was a lot of truth there, and concepts that she could apply to her own life. She wasn't considering a career change, but she had been struggling with the fact that her mother had lied to her about her adoption, and she was trying to handle that deception all on her own without any input from God.

Why hadn't her mother just simply told the truth?

Eleni didn't mind the fact that she was adopted. Plenty of people were adopted, and lived healthy and fruitful lives—in many cases, lives that would have been complete disasters if they hadn't been adopted and instead had been left in a difficult or dire situation. Being adopted even made her feel rather special. Adopted kids were chosen. Their parents didn't have to take them in and give them a home. It was an act of love. Adopted kids were truly wanted and appreciated, and adoptive parents went to great lengths to adopt a child. It was no easy process.

What bothered Eleni, however, was the lie. Was her mother so insecure that she'd thought telling the truth would put a wedge in their relationship? Or was she afraid Eleni would try to find her biological family and she would lose her relationship with her daughter? There were many possibilities, and as much as she tried to give these questions to God, she kept snatching them back and trying to figure out answers, even though some part of her realized she might never know what had motivated her mother to keep this giant secret between them.

Chris ended his call and stored his phone, then gave Eleni an intense look. "Our team has made some progress on the case."

"Anything you can share?" Eleni asked, realizing that Chris still had some limitations about what news he could actually give her about the ongoing investigation.

"This will soon be public record anyway," Chris acknowledged. "The man that we found dead today, Henry Jackson, well he had a really spotty employment record, but even so, he had apparently recently deposited a large sum of money into his bank account."

Eleni brushed some hair away from her face. "Let me guess…a payment for poisoning people at Marino's?"

"That's our guess," Chris said. "Our financial team finally finished tracing the payment, and just found that it came from Montgomery Investments, a financial firm based in New York City. Apparently, the payment was approved by a mid-level manager."

"I'd say it's time to interview that manager," Eleni said with a nod.

"I'd say the same, but it's too far to drive, and we don't have time to fly either. We could send a New York team to the office to do the interview, but I like to read a person's body language as well as listen to their verbal answers during the process."

"Looks like we need to do a video chat," Eleni said, unable to keep the enthusiasm from her voice. They finally had a lead and were making progress. The sooner they solved this case and stopped the perpetrator, the sooner her precious daughter could return home.

"Agreed, but I want a modicum of quiet when I do so." He glanced around. "Looks like we're almost back to Jackson's house. Let's do the call from the car."

It didn't take long to get back to the vehicle, or to set up the video call through a secretary at the Montgomery firm, that was thankfully still open despite the evening hour. Within minutes, they were looking at Ron Harding, a mid-level manager whose name was on the pay approval slip for Mr. Jackson.

Chris quickly introduced himself and Eleni, and then told him why they were calling. Mr. Harding asked them to wait a moment, and they could hear the keys clicking on his keyboard while he traced the payment on his laptop.

"Yes, I see the payment here. I never actually spoke

to Mr. Jackson, but according to our records, he was a private investigator located in Chicago."

"He didn't hold a license for that, Mr. Harding. What kind of work was he doing for you?" Chris asked.

"He didn't have a private investigator license?" They could hear more clicks from the keyboard. "Well, I have to admit, I find that disturbing. He must have forged his license information, because I'm looking at a license right here with the Illinois state seal." He shrugged. "Regardless, we had two prospective employees coming from the Chicago area, and Mr. Jackson was hired to do background checks on both individuals. We can't be too careful, you understand. Our firm handles large accounts with some of the biggest companies in America. We have to be able to trust our employees explicitly. You'd be surprised how many people we've caught lying on their résumés. Background checks have become routine in our human resources department. Apparently now we'll need them for our investigators as well."

"Were you the one who signed off on the payment, or were others from your firm involved?"

"Well, I routed the payment. That's part of my job. But actually, it was my boss, Wesley Montgomery, who approved the payment. He's the CEO of the corporation. I don't really know any more of the details. All I can tell you is what's on the paperwork, which is what I've already described."

Chris sighed. "The amount in question we found was twenty-five thousand dollars. Is that what you normally pay someone to do two background checks?"

There was more clicking from Mr. Harding's end. "No, that seems extremely high, but I really can't tell from this receipt if more was included or not. It's possible Mr. Jackson did some other work for us as well, but it just isn't listed on this particular slip." There was a pause from Mr. Harding, who's expression seemed troubled. "Should I be worried, Agent Springfield? Is there a problem here?"

"Mr. Jackson is dead," Chris replied. "He was found murdered today. These questions are routine, however. We're just trying to get a full understanding of what he was involved in before his death." A muscle jumped in his jaw. "Can you please send me copies of the routing paperwork? We'll need it for the file. I can provide the information where you can send it."

"Of course," Mr. Harding replied. "We're happy to comply with the FBI's request. Please let me know if I can be of further assistance."

Chris ended the call, then sent the information to Mr. Harding's phone so that the executive could send the FBI the requested records. Then he called his office and reported their findings, his tone filled with disappointment.

The same frustration Chris was exhibiting was eating at Eleni as well. The payment seemed high and Jackson had lied about being a licensed private investigator. However, without more proof of wrongdoing, or another apparent connection, they were right back where they started. Who was Henry Jackson working for, and why would he poison people through the salad bar at Marino's?

She thought back to the conversation she'd just had a few minutes ago with Chris. She knew instinctively that God wanted to be a part of every aspect of her life, not just the bits and pieces she'd decided to share with Him. And if she was completely honest with herself, she realized that she hadn't involved Him in this quest to discover the killer or his motive. She decided to fix that problem, here and now, and she closed her eyes and started praying silently. She asked God not only to help guide them in the investigation, but also to help Chris with his future plans, and to give Chris peace as he struggled with his past cases that plagued him. When she was finished, she felt invigorated and refreshed, as if God was giving her the strength to start anew.

"Yeah, looks like the Montgomery angle is a dead end."

Chris's words finally penetrated her line of thought as she heard him ending his call with his team. For some reason, even though the FBI was done with that line of inquiry, Eleni felt like the Lord was directing her to continue digging into the Montgomery family. She'd never heard of them before, and it was time to remedy that situation. Maybe it was nothing, but she was an investigative reporter, and as soon as she was in front of her computer again, she resolved to discover all she could about them. Even if she had to go down a few rabbit holes, she was going to get to the bottom of this case and bring her daughter home safely. She was sure of it.

ELEVEN

"Time's up, Chris," Tessa said through the phone, her tone exasperated. "You had your forty-eight hours, and you still don't have enough proof that Eleni Townsend is definitely the target, or her daughter. It's time to expand our focus."

"There's something here, Tessa," Chris argued as he paced the well-worn path between the dock and the back of the tiny cabin where Eleni was staying. He'd spent the last two nights on the couch, while during the day, both he and Eleni had pored over computer records, digging into Montgomery Investments, Henry Jackson, and any connection they could find between them and Eleni, Katie and Charlie. They'd found nothing. Not one shred of evidence of wrongdoing at Montgomery, and absolutely no connections that would explain the events of the past few days. "And we still can't explain why that mysterious man has been following her, or the fire that happened at her office. I'm telling you, my gut tells me there's more here. We just need enough time to figure out what's going on."

"I'd like to help you," Tessa said. "But you know

I can't. The powers that be have decided that Henry Jackson acted alone, and it was an isolated act of terrorism. You investigated a lead, and it didn't pan out. No harm no foul, but it's time to move on. We're giving the fire at Eleni's building over to the Chicago Police Department. They're investigating that separately in conjunction with the Chicago Fire Department. We're done, and it's time to move on to the next one."

Chris looked at the house, making sure Eleni was still inside and not within earshot. He moved slightly, and could see her through the window. She had given up her computer research, and was back at the boxes of her mother's things, slowly sifting through the old paperwork. He knew she was just as frustrated as he was. They'd spent hours digging into the case and had absolutely nothing to show for it.

"Eleni and Katie are still in danger. I'd bet my life on it."

"That may be true, but there's nothing we can do about it. Turn her over to CPD, and let's move on to the next case. We need evidence, not hunches."

"Come on, Tessa. We were partners. Can't you give me the benefit of the doubt?" He'd saved this card for last, hoping that reminding her of their past relationship would sway his boss. He was hesitant to mention their partnership, but these were desperate times, and he wanted to do everything in his power to keep Eleni safe.

Even so, it wasn't enough. His heart dropped when her heard her reply.

"I already did. That's why you got the forty-eight

hours in the first place. I trust your gut, Chris. You know I do. But my hands are tied."

Chris blew out a harsh breath and fisted his hands. He took a moment to compose himself, then raised the phone again. "Okay, Tessa. I understand. But you have to understand, too—I'm really worried, and am not ready to turn Eleni and Katie over to CPD. You and I both know that they'll do a few drive-bys, and that will be the end of their involvement." He ran his tongue over his teeth. "Look, I've got some personal time coming. Can I take it now?"

He could hear Tessa sigh on the other end of the line. "Are you serious? You want to take annual leave now?"

"I do," Chris confirmed. "It's that important to me."

Once again, Tessa was silent. When she spoke, her tone was firm. "Okay, Chris. As of right now, you're on leave. Come back when you're ready to hit the ground running."

"Thanks, boss," he said, meaning it. Tessa didn't have to grant his leave request, especially when she needed him in the office. She was doing him a huge favor, and they both knew it. "I'll be in touch."

"Don't get lost, Chris. I want you back as soon as you're ready. I need you here." Although her message was somewhat cryptic, Chris understood that Tessa knew he'd been struggling. He smiled to himself, glad of the camaraderie they'd shared as partners. Tessa was still like an older sister to him, even though she'd been promoted and now ran the division. He knew she cared about him, and that knowledge warmed his heart.

"I'll be in touch," he said again. "I promise." He hung up and stowed his phone, then put his hands on his hips as his eyes surveyed his surroundings. There was nothing out of the ordinary to look at, but his mind collected the details anyway. A man in a rowboat was fishing in the lake, but he was a good distance away from Eleni's tiny cabin. That wasn't unusual. There were several vacation homes nearby, and it wasn't a secret that the lake was well stocked with perch, brown trout and lake trout. He studied the man for a moment or two, but he was far away, so he couldn't learn much about him. As he watched, something glinted in the sunlight, and then the man moved his hands and quickly began reeling in a fish. A few moments later, he bent over the side of the small rowboat and used a net to bring the captured fish into the boat. There was another small reflection from the boat, and then the fisherman released the fish over the side. That wasn't unusual either. Chris knew several fishermen who practiced catch and release, especially in the lakes where some fish of certain species were known to have a high mercury content and shouldn't be eaten.

Chris wondered for a moment about the refracted light he had seen, but assumed the reflection was from the man's phone. Chris also knew fishermen who took pictures of every catch so they could tell fish stories over dinner. There didn't seem to be anything unusual or different about this fisherman. He was wearing a brown vest and a green shirt, and seemed to fit into the vacation surroundings. At least someone was having a good day. Chris was feeling more and more frustrated as the day wore on.

How was he going to solve this case? They had exhausted every lead. His entire FBI team had reached an impasse. His boss had closed the case and told him to move on. He thought over the many conversations he and Eleni had shared over the past few days, both about the case, and about their personal beliefs. Their friendship was growing, and despite the circumstances, he was appreciating their easy camaraderie and the fact that they shared so much in common, yet still had very different ideas about certain topics, which made the conversations stimulating and thought-provoking.

He was also glad they had agreed not to act on their attraction. He didn't think he'd ever be ready to pursue a long-term relationship with someone, at least not anytime soon, and was glad that the pressure to do so had been dealt with and set aside by mutual assent. He still thought she was the most beautiful woman he'd ever seen, and he caught himself watching her sometimes when she was engaged in computer research or reading an article. He enjoyed just being around her. She was a calming and positive presence. The simple things, like seeing her smile or hearing her laugh, made him happy.

He returned to the house and found Eleni still going through her mother's boxes. She had finished two more boxes last night, and had turned to another. The garbage bag had overflowed, and Eleni had opened a fourth brown paper bag and placed it by the others.

"Finding anything interesting?" he asked as he closed and locked the door behind him.

"Nothing but old bills and a few letters and birthday cards. I'm beginning to wonder if she ever threw anything away." She sighed and leaned back in her chair. "I found absolutely nothing out of the ordinary about Montgomery Investments during that last internet search, so I had to take a break. Maybe there really is nothing to find there. The company has had moderate success over the years, and seems to be a stable, well-run company. They don't take many risks, and have a solid financial base. Frankly, I can't figure out why they would be involved in anything as sordid as poisoning innocent people. Even so, I can't shake the feeling that there's something there, and I'm just missing it. I'm so frustrated, I could throw something!"

Chris gave her a smile. "I'm irritated, too, but we'll just have to start searching somewhere else. The answer has to be there. We just need to keep looking."

She gave him a smile. "Now you're encouraging me. I have to admit, Agent Springfield, we make a good team."

He laughed when she used his formal title during their banter, then glanced at her laptop. "Did you get those records about Charlie's last few clients?"

Eleni had contacted Charlie's old real estate firm, which had graciously been willing to share details about the last few transactions that Charlie had handled before his death. "I did. Nothing stood out as unusual. This is the second time I've checked. I went through everything when he died as well, and nothing stood out then either."

She paused, then slowly withdrew a small album from the bottom of the box. It had a torn and faded blue cover that had "Memories" written across it in peeling silver letters.

"What's that?" Chris asked, anxious to look at anything that wasn't a computer screen. In his book, screen fatigue was a very real phenomenon. He was definitely suffering from spending too many hours staring at the screen of his own laptop.

"Looks like an old scrapbook," Eleni replied as she opened the cover. "It's got newspaper clippings in it, and a couple of old photos. Everything is pretty faded. Several of these clippings are falling apart. This first one is from a Jacksonville paper, and it's over twenty-five years old."

"What's the headline?" Chris queried as he pulled a chair closer so they could both look at her find.

"It says 'Three-Year-Old Girl Missing, Presumed Dead,'" Eleni replied as she continued reading.

"What girl?"

"It doesn't list the girl's name. It just says that a well-known family was at the Jacksonville Beach for a family holiday in September, and their three-year-old daughter went missing during the outing. They published a picture, see?" She held out the article so he could see it, but the child was so small, it was hard to tell much about her, and the paper was faded and originally printed in black-and-white, so there was little detail to observe. Chris could see she was towheaded, Caucasian and had a pretty smile, but not much else.

"Any other articles in there about her?"

Eleni sifted through the remaining pages. "Yes, three or four more, actually. I wonder why my mother would keep such an album. I've never heard of this case. Have you?"

Chris shook his head. "Never, but it's pretty old. Hopefully, the case was solved years ago by the local authorities. What else is in that scrapbook besides the articles about the girl?"

"Ticket stubs from the Greyhound bus." She checked the dates. "Looks like my mom was in Jacksonville when the child went missing, and I was about the same age as the missing girl. What a weird coincidence. Maybe the story caught her eye when she was on vacation, and that's why she saved them. She never talked to me about visiting Florida, but she must have gone down there at least this once. If I was with her, I have no memory of it. I've spent my whole life in Chicago."

Chris shrugged. "Could be. Did she ever live in Florida?"

Eleni thumbed through some more of the book. "Not that I know of, but she talked about the state sometimes, like she knew some people that lived down there or something like that. As far as I know, she never made it out of Illinois before her death. We never traveled anywhere together when I was growing up." She turned another page. "Here's a restaurant menu from Jacksonville, and a postcard from a hotel near the beach." She tapped the card aimlessly. "My mother was never the sentimental type. I can't figure out why she would save anything from such a long-ago vacation. It's just not like her."

Chris reached for the postcard and flipped it over. "Who is Joelle Wilcox?"

Eleni leaned over and saw the name scribbled on the back of the postcard. Apparently, the card had been addressed, but never mailed. There was even an unmarked stamp in the top right-hand corner from nearly thirty years ago. "I have no idea." Even though she didn't recognize the name, she suddenly felt a cold spear of fear slide down her back. Something wasn't right here. This scrapbook was totally out of character for her mother. Saving a bunch of old bills was one thing, but old newspaper clippings about a kidnapped child? Why would her mother hold on to such a thing, and who was Joelle Wilcox?

A knot twisted in her stomach as she found the next article. She read the words out loud, "'Celia Montgomery, three-year-old daughter of Earl and Johanna Montgomery of New York City, is still missing, after getting lost during a family excursion at Jacksonville Beach one week ago. The family, including the parents, their son and their only daughter, Celia, had been vacationing in Jacksonville to celebrate the Labor Day holiday. An exhaustive search has uncovered nothing but a blanket the girl was noted for carrying with her, which was found in the surf over two miles away. The search was called off today after local authorities failed to find any more clues pointing to the child's whereabouts. Due to the tide conditions, it is thought the child wandered into the water and was pulled out to sea. She is presumed dead, although no body has been discovered.'"

"That's horrible," Chris commented softly. He went over to the couch where he had left his computer and returned shortly with the laptop in his hands. A few seconds later, he was typing furiously.

Eleni sat back in her chair, too stunned to even move. Snippets of conversations she'd had with her mother over the years that hadn't seemed to have any connection to one another suddenly snapped into place. When Chris spoke, his words only confirmed what Eleni was beginning to suspect.

"Earl Montgomery is the founder of Montgomery Investments. He died a year ago. And Johanna Montgomery died five years ago. I don't know how or why, but somehow, that family is involved in what is going on here in Chicago and your case. We've just found our missing link."

TWELVE

Chris suddenly stood, placed his laptop haphazardly on the small kitchen table and raced out the back door of the cabin. His heart was beating like a bass drum against his chest, and hadn't stopped ever since they'd discovered the Montgomery connection. His eyes scanned the horizon, but the fisherman and his boat were gone, and the lake was completely empty.

Binoculars.

When Chris had seen a flash of light, the man fishing from the rowboat hadn't been storing his phone, he'd been concealing binoculars. A phone probably wouldn't have reflected the light like he'd seen, and wasn't quite the right shape. But binoculars would have, especially smaller ones if the lens caught the light just right. And the binoculars had been pointed directly at Eleni's cabin, which means the fisherman had been watching them. He couldn't believe he'd missed it.

Fear stabbed his heart as he raced back in the house. "We have to get out of here, now," he announced as he slammed his laptop closed. "Bring the scrapbook."

Eleni looked bewildered and gave him a questioning look as he grabbed her upper arm and pulled her to her feet. "What are you talking about? We've just discovered this information about the Montgomerys, and I want to do some research to find out more."

"There's no time. You're in danger." He kept his own body between Eleni and the back of the cabin and started leading her outside. He'd lost the kidnapped child during his last case. He was going to do everything in his power to make sure he didn't lose Eleni. A wave of protectiveness surged within him.

"But we finally have a lead…" she protested. Her words were cut short by the echoing boom of a high-powered rifle round coming through the back door and imbedding itself into the wood by the bookcase. Splinters and pieces of debris went flying as a second and third bullet followed closely behind the first, both also hitting various spots of the inner wall of the cabin. Thankfully, the shooter was no expert marksman, and none of the bullets actually hit their target.

There was no time for talking or explaining. He pushed her out the front door of the cabin and toward the car as fast as he possibly could, not stopping until she was scrunching on the floorboard by the passenger-side front seat, the scrapbook tucked protectively in her arms. He circled the car at a run, then started the engine before tossing his FBI laptop in the back seat and slamming the driver-side door. "Stay down as I try to get us out of here," he said hotly.

"But my laptop and phone are still in there…" she protested.

"Yes, and that's probably how they found us," he agreed as he quickly backed the car up, did a fast three-point turn and headed down the drive. Another bullet caught the back window of the car as they escaped down the driveway. The glass splintered but didn't break, even after another round hit the rear windshield a few inches to the right. Yet another bullet hit the trunk and Chris heard the metal sing as the lead perforated the steel.

He stomped down on the accelerator and the car leaped forward, the tires grabbing purchase on the dirt and stones on the ground. They left a plume of dirt behind them as he navigated the wooded lane, quickly heading back to the main road. Trees and brush obscured his vision on both sides of the car as he raced down the drive. Chris wondered fleetingly how many criminals were chasing them, and if they were on foot, or if they would soon be pursuing them in a vehicle.

Chris didn't have long to wait. Just as he made it back to the main road, a bullet perforated the sign that advertised the cabin rental where Eleni had been staying, and another ricocheted off the back bumper. Then a blue sedan entered the road just a bit south of the drive they had been on, and another gunshot rang out. Chris wasn't sure where or even if that bullet had hit anything, but Eleni was still unharmed, huddled below, between the dashboard and the passenger seat of their car. The car was still driving, despite taking a few bullets, so Chris focused on escaping this latest attack. Eleni's safety was all he cared about.

* * *

Eleni watched as Chris pressed down again on the accelerator, speeding at an even higher velocity now that they were out on the open road. He kept both hands on the wheel as he raced down the roadway, and constantly moved his eyes between the road and the car's mirrors. The pavement turned, and it looked like it took every ounce of strength he possessed to keep the car on the road. She said a quick prayer, asking God for help as they made their escape.

"What's going on?" Eleni yelled, as she tried to steady herself by gripping the door handle. "Are they still following us?"

"They're right behind us," Chris replied, checking his rearview mirror once again.

Eleni couldn't believe how calm he sounded. Maybe he was used to being shot at, but it was a new experience for her. Fear made her muscles tense and her stomach twist. All she wanted to do was curl into a ball and scream until the danger was over. Instead, she tried to focus on his words, hoping that by talking to him, she wasn't distracting him from keeping the car on the road. "What do they look like? Is one of them that guy that has been following me?"

"I don't know. There are two men in the car—the driver and the shooter. Both are wearing baseball caps pulled low and dark glasses, so I can't identify either one. I can't even get a good glimpse of their clothes."

"What about their race, or their body types? Any clues?" she asked.

"None," he said, swerving again as the road turned

slightly. "Right before I came to get you, I saw a fisherman on the lake that looked suspicious, but I can't even tell if one of these guys is the same man or not." He grimaced. "I'm kicking myself for not realizing the danger sooner. I'm so sorry. No matter what happens, stay down and out of sight. One of them is still shooting at us. They're not giving up easily."

The highway curved again at an even steeper degree, and Eleni felt the car fishtail slightly as Chris took the turn, trying his best to stay on the road at their current rate of speed. Chris was obviously a very skilled driver, and she was glad that she wasn't the one behind the wheel. Driving down the streets of Chicago was one thing—but driving with a shooter on their tail was quite another matter. Without Chris at the wheel, she would have already been dead.

A huge crash suddenly sounded behind them, and she could barely make out a large cloud of black smoke from her vantage point on the floorboard.

"That sounded bad! What happened?" she asked.

"Looks like the driver miscalculated how fast he could go around that last bend," he said, the relief evident in his voice. "They just crossed the double yellow line and ended up in the ditch on the other side of the road. There's smoke pouring out of the engine. I think they're done chasing us—at least for now."

Eleni felt Chris slow the vehicle some and she said a quick prayer of thankfulness. She started to get up into the passenger seat, but Chris motioned for her to stay put. "Just sit tight for another few minutes. Please. I know you're uncomfortable down there, but rifles have long ranges, and I want you well out of the shooter's sites before you get in that seat." He pulled out his phone and quickly reported the incident, then stowed his phone, his eyes still scanning the surrounding area.

"Are you sure they can't still be following us?"

"Positive," he replied. He motioned to Eleni with his hand. "Okay, you can get up in the seat now, and please put on your seat belt."

"Yeah, I think a seat belt sounds like an excellent idea," she agreed. "Should we go back and check on them?" she asked as she pulled herself up and clicked her seat belt. "I'm not anxious to get shot, but I don't want to leave someone bleeding out by the side of the road either, and you're armed, right?"

"Not a chance," Chris replied firmly. "I'm armed, but the sniper was using a high-powered rifle, similar to what I used during my army days. It has an incredible range, and my little pistol isn't even in the same league." He visibly relaxed a bit and ran his hand through his hair. "Since you seem to be their target, I'm not letting you get anywhere close to them, even if they are injured. That's the price they'll have to pay." He glanced in the rearview mirror once more. "I'm fairly sure the perps' vehicle was totaled in the crash. And that car they were driving is a newer model, so it probably had front and side airbags. They'll be hurting, but local law enforcement should be able to take care of them shortly and get them any medical assistance they may need. I doubt very seriously that their lives will be in danger if they have to wait a few minutes for the emergency personnel to arrive."

Eleni took a calming breath, then forced herself to release the door handle that she'd been grasping with a white-knuckled grip. Her heart was still hammering against her chest, even though they were now going a normal rate of speed and the pursuit and danger seemed to be over. "You saved my life back there, Chris. Thank you. If I'd been out here by myself, I'd be dead right now." She reached over and touched his arm and gave it a gentle squeeze, then withdrew.

Chris glanced in her direction, obviously uncomfortable with her thanks. "Well, at least we've confirmed you're the target, and we know that whoever wants to hurt you is now willing to take direct action against you instead of obscuring his purpose by hurting a group. I guess that's progress of a sort. We might even be able to get the FBI involved again. This act alone should be enough to convince my boss that you're the true target."

"We know more than that," she agreed pensively. "We've also found the connection to the Montgomery family."

"We need to spend some more time digging on the internet and see if we can figure out the connection," Chris replied. "Now that we have another lead to follow, we might just get to the bottom of this."

Eleni still gripped the scrapbook, and now that they were going a normal speed, she opened it again and continued thumbing through it. Suddenly her heart stopped and a knot instantly formed in her stomach. An image stared back at her from the page—one she hadn't seen for many, many years.

"Are you okay?" Chris asked.

Eleni glanced over and saw the worry in his eyes. She wondered if her own distress was as transparent. "Can you please pull over?"

He nodded and searched for a safe spot to pull onto the highway's shoulder. About five miles later, they came to a place with a historical sign by the side of the road that allowed drivers to stop and learn about a past event. Chris did a fast parking job, but left the engine running.

Eleni looked around the area and was instantly glad they were alone. She lifted the book and showed him the article she had found in the scrapbook. It was in better shape than the other articles, and seemed to be from a more recent edition of a newspaper. In the center of the article, there was an age-progressed photo of the missing girl, Celia Montgomery.

"This looks just like my seventh grade school photo," she said quietly. "I think I'm that missing girl."

THIRTEEN

"So, you're Celia Montgomery, the one and only daughter of Earl and Johanna Montgomery?" Tessa asked, her eyebrow raised.

"It's certainly possible," Eleni replied, still trying to come to terms with the revelation herself. She showed the age-progressed photo from the newspaper article to Chris's boss. "I only recently found out I was adopted. My mother died a few months ago, and she never mentioned it, or how the adoption came about, so I honestly don't know what to think. It's something we need to explore, at any rate. I'm sure we'd need a DNA test to prove anything conclusively." They had returned to FBI headquarters in downtown Chicago, and had reported directly to Tessa upon arrival. Chris had been quick to fill his boss in on what they had discovered, how they had been watched at the cabin and their narrow escape from the shooter. Tessa had immediately contacted the local law enforcement and confirmed that both men who had been chasing them had minor injuries from the crash and had been arrested, but both had lawyered up immediately without making any statements, incriminating or otherwise.

"If it's true," Eleni continued, "it would explain a lot of my childhood. But I'm not sure what to do next, or how it ties into this case. I certainly don't want anything from that family. I mean, I don't even know them. But if I am Celia, and we can prove it, then I would think they'd want some closure so at least they'd know I survived after whatever happened all those years ago on that Jacksonville beach." She rubbed her arms in a soothing motion, trying to wrap her head around this latest revelation. "I'm sorry Johanna and Earl Montgomery are already dead. If I am their missing child, they both died before knowing that I'm still alive. That's incredibly sad."

"Well, what did happen?" Chris asked. "Do you have any memory of the events described in the newspaper articles?"

"I don't remember it at all, but the child who went missing was only three. That explains a lot." Eleni leaned back in her chair. "My mother never wanted to answer questions about who my father was, so I always assumed I was born out of wedlock and the truth embarrassed her, or that I was a child of rape. In any case, my mother never spoke about any of this. She told me her parents had died before I was born, and I never met any aunts or uncles. Any time I asked her anything about our family, she avoided the questions, so eventually, I quit asking." She went on to explain how she had discovered that she was adopted after her mother's death, and that her mother had never told her the truth about her parentage. "Honestly, I'm a bit concerned about my mother's involvement in the kidnapping. We found another name on a postcard—Joelle Wilcox. But I don't know who that woman is, or what role she played in the abduction, if any." She shrugged. "I may never know."

Tessa listened to all of this and appeared to come to a quick conclusion. "So, the Montgomery family paid Henry Jackson, a man claiming to be a private eye, twenty-five thousand to poison the food at Marino's Deli. Is that our working theory?"

"That's it in a nutshell," Chris agreed.

"Why?" She tapped her cheek in a pensive motion. "If you are the missing child, why would they want you dead?"

Eleni and Chris looked at each other, and they both shrugged.

"That's what we still don't know," Chris replied. "We know there's a connection, but right when we discovered the newspaper articles and were getting ready to research the issue, the perps started shooting at us."

"Alright," Tessa said, clearly thinking through every aspect of what they did and didn't know regarding this case. Eleni was very impressed with this woman, and liked her immediately. She was straightforward and down-to-earth, and was a consummate professional, through and through. "Let's get you both in front of a computer. Let me know when you have more." She nodded at Chris. "Looks like you're back on the clock."

"Yes, ma'am," he responded as she left them by Chris's desk.

"What does that mean?" Eleni asked, once Tessa was out of earshot.

Chris shrugged. "I was taking personal time to investigate this case with you. Now that we have a new lead that proves you're in danger, the FBI is back on board."

Eleni felt a rush of emotion at his statement, but humbleness topped the list. "I hadn't realized you were making such a sacrifice for me. Thank you." She could tell she'd embarrassed him by her words. He flushed and even the tips of his ears reddened a bit. It was very endearing. The more time she spent with him, the more he seemed like a giant teddy bear. He could be tough when it was warranted, but was usually gentle and shy. His softer side made her like him even more.

"You're welcome," he responded quietly, then quickly turned to the computer. "Let's see what else we can find."

She smiled and let him change the subject. Although she hadn't changed her mind about keeping their relationship on a purely friendship level, there were times over the last few days when the attraction had still sprung up between them, and now was one of them. Still, there was no way she was going to trust her heart with someone new. It simply hurt too much when that person was torn away—and she didn't think she could survive another loss. Charlie's death had been devastating. She didn't wish that kind of pain on anyone, and certainly didn't want to open herself up to the possibility of experiencing it again by giving her heart away. No, it was better and safer to stay single and focus on Katie. That would be enough. It would have to be.

"Check this out," Chris said as he pointed to his screen and pulled her out of her woolgathering. "Here's a picture of the Montgomery family about seven years ago from the company website."

Eleni pulled up a chair, sat down and studied the photo. She felt like she'd been running a marathon the last few hours, and was ready to take a break and really dig into this new and possible revelation about her past. Earl Montgomery was a dignified-looking man, with gray hair and deep creases on his face. His wife, Johanna, had a stately appearance as well, and seemed to be classy and sophisticated. Despite their apparent success and bearing, they also both seemed to have an air of sadness portrayed in the photo. But what really caught Eleni's attention was the other man standing behind the couple in the picture. He appeared to be in his early twenties, and looked like he had just finished running a board meeting. He had short dark hair, pleasant features and a confident smile.

He was also the man that had been following Eleni, and who had approached Katie at the hospital.

A cold chill swept down Eleni's spine. "That's him. That's the guy that's been following me." She scanned the photo's caption. "His name is Zach Montgomery." She turned and her eyes locked with Chris's. "That means, if I really am Celia Montgomery, my own brother is trying to kill me."

"I'd say, it's time to track down Zach Montgomery and bring him in for questioning," Chris said firmly. During the course of his career, he'd seen family members turn on each other, but this situation seemed incredibly strange to him. If Eleni really was Celia Montgomery, she'd had no idea, and hadn't been trying to contact the family, or establish any sort of relationship with them. So, what possible motive could Zach have for trying to kill her? And why hurt all of those other people so indiscriminately? Were the collateral damages so insignificant to Zach that he really didn't care who got hurt or killed, as long as his objective was achieved?

"I agree," Eleni said quietly. "We need to find him and lock him in a room until we get answers."

Chris noticed her subdued tone and gave her a playful nudge. "Hey. Don't worry. We're going to figure this out."

"I know," Eleni said. "This is just a lot for me to absorb at one time. This morning, I was just Eleni Townsend, reporter, with not much of a history. Now my life is suddenly filled with intrigue. I've got to tell you, I think I was a lot happier before I knew about this possible connection to the Montgomery family."

"Because of the murders, or because of something else?"

Eleni grimaced. "The murders are a big part of it. I hate to think that other people were hurt and killed because I am apparently the target of some vendetta or problem that I don't even really understand. But I'm also hurt to know this information about my mother." She sat back in her chair. "Was she the kidnapper? It certainly seems that way since she was in Jacksonville herself at the time of the crime. But even if she didn't actually steal me from the beach that day, she certainly must have known what happened and how I came to be her daughter." Her expression turned bleak. "How could she have done such a thing?"

Chris squeezed her hand, then released it. "We don't know all the facts yet. Let's wait and see what we discover. I have a feeling you're going to learn a lot over the next few days." He handed her his cell phone. "Look. I'm going to try to keep researching this. Why don't you use my phone and give Katie a call? It might really do you some good to hear her voice."

Eleni gave him a grateful smile. "What a good idea. Thanks!" She took the phone, stood and moved away so she could get a bit more privacy. She'd been worried about not having her own phone in case there was an emergency with Katie, and hearing the child's voice would help reassure her immeasurably.

Chris watched her go, his heart hurting for her. Although he was dealing with his own issues and possible career changes, he couldn't imagine dealing with finding out your entire history was based on a lie and probable criminal activity. His own parents had been wonderful people and mentors. Although no parent was perfect, his childhood had been wonderful, and he had no complaints. They certainly hadn't stolen him from another family or concealed his true identity.

He glanced over at Eleni, who was speaking to her daughter in a caring and animated way. Her body language had changed, and the stressful way she had been carrying herself was now replaced with happiness and pleasure. He could easily see that the call had rejuvenated her, despite the revelations of the day. Eleni was a devoted parent. It was obvious in the way she fought for her daughter's safety—and how she did whatever was necessary to protect her, even at great personal sacrifice.

His thoughts returned to what she had learned about her mother. How did a person forgive someone, especially a loved family member, after such duplicity? He needed to get to work, but he took a moment to look up a Bible verse first. He knew there was a verse somewhere about needing to forgive someone seven times seventy, and he found what he was looking for in Matthew, chapter 18. There was no ambiguity, yet he struggled with the concept, and said a short prayer for her.

God, please be with Eleni as she deals with this news about her childhood, and help her work through the feelings and issues this raises within her. Help her forgive her mom and anyone else that might have been involved in her kidnapping. Also, please help us solve this crime before anyone else gets hurt, and bring justice to the families of all of the victims. Amen.

Even though he had been praying for Eleni and

not himself, he felt a sense of peace sweep over him. He knew that God had heard his prayer and would be helping her through this difficult situation. Chris knew it with absolute certainty.

But why did he have trouble asking God to help him with his own struggles? It was a paradox. He was happy to pray for others, but hesitated to ask God for help for himself. Yet he knew God wanted him to pray, and communicate with Him about every aspect of his life, just as Eleni had suggested during their walk the other day. He'd realized more and more over the last couple of days that he had been shutting God out of his worries and concerns, and had been trying to handle everything on his own. That had been a big mistake. He decided to rectify the problem right now. He closed his eyes and said another prayer, this time asking God to forgive him for pulling away from Him, and asking Him to come back into his life and to help guide him in His perfect will.

The result was electrifying, and helped him feel even better about the doubts and career choices that he was facing. He knew he still needed to make some decisions about his future, but he also knew that he wasn't going to take another step forward without asking God to direct his steps.

He turned back to his keyboard, refreshed, and started searching for "Zach Montgomery." It was easy to find an address for him in New York City where Montgomery Investments operated and, apparently, he was one of the vice presidents of the company, in charge of procurements and contracting. They had

seen the man in Chicago several times since the poisoning, but his home was in New York.

Where was he staying in Chicago? Hopefully, he
wouldn't be that hard to track down if he was still in
the city.

He stood and went in search of Tessa to see if they
had enough for an arrest warrant. The conversation
was short and sweet. She supported sending a New
York team to interview him, but believed that since
they had no direct evidence of wrongdoing, there
wasn't enough yet for an arrest. Chris grudgingly
agreed. Though they had observed him following
Eleni, they hadn't actually caught Zach Montgomery doing something criminal. Being in the same
location where crimes had been committed was suspicious, but wasn't proof of anything illegal. They
needed more, but at least now they had a direction
and focus for the investigation. That was much more
than they'd had when the day had started. He called
his contact at the New York office and did the formal request for that FBI office to find Montgomery
and do the interview.

As he was hanging up the phone, Eleni returned
and sat down next to him, a smile of happiness on
her face. "That was just what the doctor ordered,"
she said as she leaned back in her chair. She handed
him back his phone.

"How's Katie doing?"

"She's barely sat still since she went to stay with
my friends. They've got two kids of their own, and
they homeschool, so Katie has been learning and hav-

ing a great time with their co-op. Today they visited a bakery to see how they made bread. The baker made quite the impression, and gave them each a choice of cookies or doughnuts, and then let them decorate them." She sighed. "She's all sugared up, happy as can be. She's decided she wants to be a baker, too, when she grows up." She brushed some hair away from her face. "I was worried this whole experience was going to traumatize her, but she seems to be bouncing back really well. This is one big adventure for her."

"Kids are pretty resilient," Chris agreed. "I'm glad you got to connect. I know it's hard for you to be separated like this, but it sounds like she's doing great." He set his phone down by his keyboard and motioned toward his computer. "We can't get an arrest warrant for Zach Montgomery, but we're sending over a team to his New York house to ask him some questions." Before he could explain more, his phone rang and he raised a finger, asking Eleni to wait while he answered it. He had a short conversation, then hung up and met Eleni's eye. "Well, that was an interesting piece of news." He tilted his head. "Zach Montgomery is still in Chicago. According to his secretary, he's staying at the Intercontinental Hotel downtown." He stood. "I think it's time we paid him a little visit. Agreed?"

Eleni stood, too. "Agreed. Let's go."

FOURTEEN

It was shortly past five thirty in the evening when Eleni and Chris parked their car in a nearby garage and headed over to the Intercontinental Hotel. Thankfully, some of the five o'clock traffic had started to ebb, but the roads were still a quagmire of vehicles, and it had taken them longer than expected to reach their destination and find a place to park that was in walking distance of the hotel.

Chris wasn't thrilled to have Eleni with him as they headed to confront Zach Montgomery, and he'd tried to talk her out of coming during the entire ride over from the FBI building. Even so, his concerns had fallen on deaf ears. Eleni would not be dissuaded, and convinced him that she would follow him over regardless of whether or not they rode together in the same vehicle. She wanted answers, and she was determined to get them.

As a result, trepidation flowed through him. This was why victims shouldn't be involved in investigations. He knew the concept well, but was also doing his best to protect her. With her determination to solve the case, with or without him, he knew he had the best chance of keeping her safe if he kept her close by. Eleni was an investigative reporter with a drive to find the truth that just didn't stop. She would surely get in his way if he didn't have her near him. Still, he couldn't stop the worry and fear for her safety. He had lost his last victim, and the kidnapped child's murder would haunt him forever. He couldn't lose Eleni, too.

What would he do if Eleni was harmed?

The thought made him sick to his stomach, warning him that he was getting too close, even though he felt powerless to pull back. There was something special about this woman that he could not deny, regardless of their pledge to remain only friends. Her smile made his heart speed up. The caring in her eyes made him feel strong, like he could conquer the world.

They walked down the sidewalk, stepping around a group of tourists taking pictures with the famous Chicago architecture behind them, and also passing two dog walkers that each held several leashes' worth of canines in various sizes, shapes and colors.

The first bullet whizzed by Chris's head and slammed into the greystone building behind him, making a sizable divot while exploding bits of rock and debris flew through the air. He instinctively ducked, and pulled Eleni down with him, then sought the nearest cover. There wasn't much around that they could hide behind. With few choices available, he pulled her over behind a concrete planter that the city had filled with brightly colored petunias and tulips.

The second bullet hit the ground near where they

had been standing only seconds before. The lead rico-cheted off the pavement, shattering the glass display window of a store that offered a variety of Chicago tourist items for sale. Another bullet struck a man-nequin dressed in a Chicago T-shirt and shorts, car-rying a tote bag with the Willis Tower and the Navy Pier Centennial Wheel emblazoned on the side. One leg disintegrated as it took the brunt of the bullet, and the plastic form tilted awkwardly to the left, slipping dangerously close to a shelf displaying several glass paperweights and a rack of sunglasses.

Chaos ensued. The sound of the gunshots sent peo-ple running in various directions, even though they didn't know where the shooter was, or where to find safety. Chris heard screaming, dogs barking and car horns sounding as the people scrambled to get away from the gunshots. He stayed focused on Eleni, his weapon pulled and his body shielding hers the best he could. They huddled together, so close that he could smell the mint on her breath and the lavender on her skin. Her eyes had rounded and her face had paled, making her gray eyes stand out like shards of gray labradorite.

"Are you okay?" she whispered, her voice shaking.

"So far," he responded. "Are you?"

"Yes," she said, nodding.

"Good. Stay down and stay still." His eyes scanned the area. It was a waste to return fire. He had no target to aim at and imagined that the rifleman was in one of the buildings across the street, shooting from one of the higher windows. Just like at the cabin by the lake, Chris knew his pistol had a limited range, and could do little against a high-powered rifle. This area of downtown Chicago was also very congested, and he doubted he could even shoot cover fire to move from their current location without putting innocent people in danger, which he absolutely refused to do. They were essentially pinned down, and if the shooter moved to find a better angle or if there was more than one gunman out there, he knew they didn't have much of a chance to survive. He felt like a sitting duck. He pulled his phone and reported the incident, making sure they knew there was a plainclothes law enforcement officer on the scene. Then he stowed it again, his eyes still searching for a way to get Eleni to safety.

He began to pray, even as his eyes continued to scan the windows of the apartment buildings opposite them, hoping for some sort of sign where the shooter was scoping them from. He saw nothing—no rifle barrel, no curtain moving. Nothing.

Sirens sounded in the distance. As they started to grow in volume, two more bullets hit the planter they were hiding behind. Slivers of concrete flew into the air, proving the sniper knew where they were hiding and was determined to wait them out. Eleni yelped, but stayed in a tight ball behind the concrete. Chris wanted to shout in frustration. He felt so helpless— so vulnerable. He moved slightly, apparently giving the shooter a better target, and another bullet whizzed by his shoulder, missing him by a hair. This rifleman was obviously much more skilled than the one who had tried to shoot them at the cabin. But Chris was getting tired of being a target, and wanted Eleni to be holed up somewhere secure until this case was concluded. If he had anything to say about it, she wouldn't be accompanying him for any more interviews. She needed to be in a safe house, hidden away and guarded 24/7 so the killers couldn't keep taking shots at her. He wanted—no, he *needed* to keep her protected.

The minutes slowly ticked by. Perspiration popped out on his brow, and his muscles tensed as the emotions swirled within him.

Finally, the sirens got even louder, and suddenly several police cars arrived on the scene, coming from both directions. Chris moved again, but there was no answering gunfire, and he breathed a sigh of relief. With this many law enforcement officers on the scene, the shooter had probably decided it was time to make his escape.

Chris moved again and caught Eleni's eye. "See that alley there?" He nodded to a narrow space between the Intercontinental's side door and a loading area where the hotel received deliveries, and she nodded. "Good. When I say go, you run there as fast as you can. I'll be right behind you."

"Okay, Chris."

The look of confidence in her eyes bolstered him even more and he squeezed her hand, then released it. "Let's do it. Ready? Go!"

She jumped up and starting running toward the loading dock, and he followed close behind her, making sure to keep his body between Eleni and where he believed the gunman had been camouflaged. She slipped slightly on some wet bricks, and he grabbed her arm and helped her maintain her balance. It only took them a few seconds to reach their destination, and no further bullets rang out as they leaned against the wall of the loading area, well out of sight from the road and the shooter's possible site. Chris felt like this was a much safer place to be. He pulled Eleni close, thankful that they had survived this latest brush with death. She fit perfectly in his arms and for a moment, he just relished the closeness. "We can wait here until the police clear the scene."

"Yes, that would be a good idea."

Chris instantly released Eleni and spun around at the sound of the threatening voice. A large burly man wearing black pants and a gray shirt, was standing only a few feet away, holding a .45 pistol on both of them. He had short dark hair and a ragged scar on his right cheek, but Chris didn't recognize his features. The empty look in the man's eyes and the grim smirk on his face was enough to show that he was a dangerous adversary. Chris quickly pushed Eleni behind him, and then he saw the second man, also large and brawny, step out of the shadows. This one was wearing jeans and a dark blue shirt advertising the Chicago Bears. He had a tattoo of a tiger on his forearm, and in his right hand, a 9 mm pistol, also pointed directly at them. He had such broad shoulders, Chris actually wondered if the man used to play linebacker for the Bears before he moved into a life of crime.

"Now, why don't you take your gun out of your

holster, there, nice and slow. Then put it on the ground and kick it over to me," the newer man said, his voice low and ominous. "Use your index finger and your thumb," he continued. "If I see you do anything else, I'll shoot you both."

"I'm with the FBI," Chris said quietly, hoping to resolve this conflict before it escalated, "and this woman is under my protection. You don't want to hurt either one of us."

"That's where you're wrong," the first man said as he raised one side of his mouth in a sardonic smile. "Law enforcement doesn't scare me. And to be completely honest, I don't really care whether we hurt you or not. One cop's the same as any other in my book. But the woman there, well, there's a price on her head, and she'll be dead by sundown. That's a promise."

Chris gritted his teeth, the man's words chilling him to the bone. He glanced around the area, but even though cops would soon be swarming around, right here and now, they were alone with these two thugs, and he was at a definite disadvantage. He took a step back, then another, pushing Eleni backward as he did so. Stalling was the only tactic that came to mind. "Why? She's done nothing to you. And you can still walk away. If you shoot either one of us, the other cops will be here in seconds and they'll be on you like glue."

"No one's walking away, buddy," the Bears fan declared, "unless it's you." He took a step toward them. "You're outnumbered, and no matter how fast you pull, you won't get us both before we get the two of you." He smiled, revealing tobacco-stained teeth that made him look even more malicious. "Now put down your weapon, like I said, and you might actually survive this day."

Eleni couldn't stop trembling. She was going to die, here, in this filthy loading dock, for reasons she still didn't understand. It was maddening. Both thugs held themselves with calm assurance that they would win this battle of wills, and there were two of them, and only one of Chris. Even at his best, there was no way he could get them both without one of them returning fire. She glanced at the deadly weapons in their hands and shuddered. Neither of them had a silencer on their guns, but there were blaring sirens and so much street noise that she wondered if it really mattered. Cops would come to investigate, but they would be too late. By the time they searched for the source of the shooting, she'd be dead.

What she didn't want was for Chris to die here with her. The Bible verse from John suddenly flashed through her mind. *Greater love hath no man than this, that a man lay down his life for his friends.* She suddenly realized that her feelings for Chris went beyond friendship, even though she had denied it to herself and to him, over and over again. She loved him. She couldn't watch him die, not if she could stop it. They clearly only wanted her. This might be her only chance to save him. "If I come with you quietly, will you let him live?"

Scarface smiled, showing a silver tooth on the left

side of his mouth. "How sweet. The lady wants to bar-
gain."

Chris shook his head and took another step back,
and Eleni was now wedged between him and the brick
wall behind her. There was literally no place else for
her to go. "No, Eleni. Don't do it. I won't let you sacrifice yourself for me," Chris said softly for her ears
alone. "And they can't be trusted. They're going to
shoot me regardless of what they promise."

"I'm done talking," Scarface said roughly, raising
his voice. "Put your gun on the ground now, or face
the consequences."

"You're not getting the woman," Chris said, his
voice equally firm. "And I'm a really good shot. The
only question is, which one of you will die first." He
motioned with his head toward Scarface. "My guess
is it will be you. You're the one hoping for the big
payday, so you'll get paid alright. In a way you never
expected." He asked the Bears fan, "How much did
he promise you to come along? Probably only a tenth
of the total amount he's hoping to get paid. He'll get
rich, and you'll get the leftovers."

The Bears fan sent a suspicious look over to Scarface, and Eleni saw Chris's hand slowly move toward
his hip. Eleni could tell from her protector's body language that he had absolutely no intention of following
their directions or giving up his gun. He was going
to die for her, or they were going to die together, and
there wasn't a single thing she could do about it. She
felt helpless and nauseated. She was going to lose

him, just like she had lost Charlie. Her skin felt suddenly cold, and she stiffened, the fear paralyzing her.

Suddenly, there was a new voice in the mix, and she turned slightly to see who had spoken in a cool, commanding tone.

"Leave them both alone. Now."

Zach Montgomery had walked up silently from behind the group. He didn't appear to have a gun like the others, but his presence alone made the terror in Eleni escalate even further, and her heart plummeted. This man had been following her, and had appeared nearly every time her life had been in danger over the last several days. If he was here now, and willing to show himself, then their chances of survival must be nonexistent. Yet if what she'd learned today was true, wasn't he also her brother? How could a brother hunt down and murder his only sibling? It was barbaric. It was insane. Yet it was playing out right in front of her.

Her thoughts scattered as Scarface turned his weapon on the newcomer. "I've got my orders. It was made very clear to me that I don't get paid unless the job gets done, and gets done right this time." He sneered at Zach. "You're not even the one paying my fee. I'll take you out, too, if that's what it takes for me to get my money."

Zach didn't back down. "I'm giving you new orders. If you want to see even a dime of what you were promised, you'll do as I say."

FIFTEEN

The two thugs had both turned their attention to Zach, and Chris chose that moment to act while they were distracted. The man with the scar was closer, only a couple of steps away, and still had his weapon pointed at Chris's midriff. Chris quickly closed the distance between them, then used his left hand to grab the top of the man's gun and push it away from them so the barrel pointed to the side. Then he used his right hand to turn the gun's barrel again so it was now pointed back at the hit man. He could hear the man's thumb break as the perp tried in vain to maintain control and his grip on the weapon. Then Chris moved even closer, grabbed the gun and pulled it out of Scarface's hand.

The entire movement was over in only a few seconds, but the Bears fan was well-trained and responded quickly to Chris's actions. He immediately took a few steps closer and swung out with his arm, hitting Chris on the temple with his own weapon. Chris staggered from the blow, but managed to fire at Scarface, who was still standing directly in front of him. The lead hit the offender square in the chest, causing a circle of red to bloom on his shirt. The light dimmed in the man's eyes, and then disappeared completely as his body slumped to the ground.

Chris felt a trickle of blood sliding down near his ear from the wound, but kept on his feet, even though his head was pounding from the blow. He saw the Bears fan move his leg, but wasn't able to move fast enough to avoid the kick that hit his hand and sent the .45 handgun flying through the air. It landed well out of his reach, several feet away, and he heard the metal slide against the asphalt. Before he could reach for his own weapon that was still holstered, the perp moved in closer, hitting Chris with a hard fist to the gut.

Chris staggered, grunted in pain and struggled to breathe. He heard Eleni cry out behind him and turned his head to see what was happening. Zach had reached for her, and was pulling her by her arm away from the fray.

"No!" Chris called out, his voice rough. He reached out to try to help her, but that only gave the Bears fan another opportunity to attack. The felon reached out again with his gun hand, but instead of shooting him, he hit Chris in the head again, this time sending him to the ground. Then he pulled his foot back and gave Chris a vicious kick.

"Stay down," the man ordered.

Pain radiated through Chris's ribs, and he curled into a ball, trying to protect himself from the giant of a man that was attacking him. He reached for his own gun again, and actually managed to get it into his hand, but as soon as he did so, the other man kicked it away as well.

The Bears fan still had his own gun in his hand, and he turned it on Eleni, pointing it at her chest. She screamed, and Chris quickly reached out to stop him, but he was only able to grasp the man's boot. He kicked Chris's hand away and maintained his aim on Eleni. Chris reached for him again, but was still on the ground just out of reach and powerless to help her.

Chris's vision swam as he struggled to stay conscious. The last thing he remembered seeing was Zach Montgomery stepping in front of Eleni as the gunman fired, and Zach crumpling to the ground, only a few feet away from him, his shoulder covered in blood.

Eleni screamed as Chris went down, and shrieked again when Zach got shot and crumpled at her feet. Chris wasn't moving! She reached for him and tried to get to his side, but before she could even touch him, the gunman viciously grabbed her arm and pulled her away. The man was a giant, and his grip was like steel. She had no way to escape.

"Look, lady," the man said under his breath. "Right now, they're both alive and breathing. If you don't want that to change, shut your mouth and come with me. Understand?"

On some level, Eleni did realize that both Chris and Zach had been left alive, but the man with the scar on his face had no doubt died the moment the bullet had entered his chest. Zach was moaning, and although he was moving slightly, she knew there was nothing he could do to stop her abductor. Chris was silent, but she hadn't seen him get shot. She thought the repeated blows to the head had probably knocked him unconscious. Even though he had been injured in other ways as well, she thought he was probably still alive. Her heart ached for him, yet on some level, the criminal's words penetrated her brain and she decided not to fight him. If she allowed him to take her away, the other two men had at least a chance to survive. If she didn't, she had no doubt that this mountain of a man would shoot them both, making sure they would both die right then and there in front of her. She knew her own chances of survival were slim to nonexistent, but if she had even a small chance to save Chris, and her brother, too, she had to take it. She didn't know Zach's story, or what was really going on, but she had seen Zach take a bullet for her with her own eyes. His actions raised all sorts of questions in her mind—questions that she may never find the answers to, especially since her time left was obviously limited. Regardless, Zach's actions spoke louder than words, and she didn't want him dead.

"Okay. I'll do whatever you say. Just please don't hurt them anymore."

The man grunted in response, but his grip loosened somewhat once he seemed to realize he had her cooperation. He pulled her deeper into the alley, and after a short distance, they walked into another section of the loading area where there was a gray sedan parked. He unlocked the vehicle and pushed her into the front passenger side, then circled the car and settled into the driver's seat. She dared not try to escape. They were still too close to Chris and Zach, and she didn't want to take any chances that this man would go back and finish them off if she didn't follow his directions explicitly. Even so, escape was foremost in her mind, and she considered various possibilities as her abductor turned to her and duct-taped her wrists together, then ripped the end of the tape from the roll with his fingers.

"Just in case you get any crazy ideas," he said gruffly. "I'm not sure what I'm going to do with you yet, so for now, just sit there and stay quiet, or I'll tape your mouth shut as well."

She nodded, not wanting to make him any angrier. He seemed like he was already simmering and near the boiling point. She'd never seen this man before, and although he had shown some compassion by not murdering Chris and her brother outright, she didn't want to push him any further and test his patience until she had a clear plan of escape. He still had a loaded weapon in his pocket, and his demeanor and expression made it very clear that he was on the edge and could be pushed into even more violence with very little provocation.

He started the engine and pulled away from the curb, and only a few minutes later they had entered the flow of traffic on one of the major Chicago thoroughfares. He'd managed to avoid the jam of police and vehicles that swarmed over the Intercontinental, and although they passed several police heading in that direction, they had no trouble going the opposite way. Eleni's heart sank as they got farther and farther away from the downtown area. By now, she was sure paramedics were caring for both Chris and Zach, but she still worried about their conditions. She doubted she would ever see either one of them again, and her chest hurt with the realization.

And what about her darling Katie? Tears welled in her eyes. Who would take care of her daughter? She had made a will and named guardians at Katie's birth, but she'd honestly never thought she would need to use them. Was the call she'd made this afternoon really the last chance she'd ever have to talk to her daughter? She tried her best not to cry, but couldn't stop a sob that broke from her lips.

He abductor wasn't pleased, and reached out and slapped her face. "I said no talking. That meant no noise either. I need to think. Just sit there, and stay quiet. Got it?"

She nodded, her cheek still stinging from the blow. She had no illusions about the man's intentions. He was going to kill her. It was just a matter of time.

They drove southwest for about an hour until they were clear of the city and the land gave way to farms and woodland. Even the traffic thinned and ebbed as they made their way on backcountry roads. A few minutes later, her abductor turned onto a rutted dirt road that ended in a small driveway by a cabin. It was similar in size and shape to the house by the lake where she had been staying before, but that's where the similarities ended. This one was obviously not used as a rental property, and was in a state of total disrepair. Peeling paint was coming off the front door, the porch and the railings, and a broken porch swing, covered in old leaves and spiderwebs, stood in front of the one window that was murky with mold. Overgrown plants and weeds surrounded the building, giving the property an even stronger feeling of abandonment.

The Bears fan seemed totally unaffected by the condition of the cabin and parked to the side under a leaning carport. He shut off the engine and turned to Eleni. "We can do this the easy way, or the hard way. The choice is up to you."

Eleni dared not ask any questions, but her terror was palpable. Was he going to hurt her first, or just kill her outright? She didn't know what to expect, and her imagination was already running through various scenarios. She knew for a fact he was bigger and stronger than she was. If she had any hope of escaping, she would have to bide her time and wait for the perfect opportunity, and she might only get one chance to make a break for it. She glanced at his face and furrowed brow, trying to read him. How much time did she actually have left?

The large man got out of the car, then came over and pulled her out by the arm, jerking her to her feet. Without another word, he led her up the steps to the cabin's front door, unlocked it and pushed her inside.

There was only a bit of light coming in through the front window, but the inside of the building wasn't much better than the outside. A thick layer of dust had settled on everything, including the couch and two chairs that framed an old TV sitting on a rickety stand with a silver antenna poking out from the top. There were no pictures on the walls, but they were papered in a water-stained design of green trees and bears on a faded yellow background. A stack of old magazines filled two milk crates near the couch, and old, dirty dishes were stacked on a couple of TV trays on a threadbare carpet.

Eleni wrinkled her nose as the smell of mold and rotting food met her nostrils. The sour odor made her stomach churn, but she made a herculean effort to keep her reaction as minimal as possible. She did not want to anger her captor in any way, knowing that he was already on the edge.

Would this hovel be the last place she ever saw in her life? In her mind's eye, she pictured her sweet Katie, a smile on her face, with sticky fingers and a light in her eyes. Somehow, she had to survive. Katie was depending on her.

Her thoughts moved to Chris, her gentle giant. She hadn't even had a chance to tell him that she loved him. Would she die before she could express her true feelings for him?

Her reverie was interrupted when the man pulled her toward the hallway, then pushed her into a small bedroom that had only a bare twin mattress and a rickety, wooden end table. He turned her to face him and sliced the tape from her wrists with a sharp pocketknife. Then he closed the door behind her and locked it from the outside without saying a word. Escape still weighed heavy on her mind, and she immediately explored the small space as she rubbed her hands together, trying to get the feeling back in them.

There wasn't much to see. There was no other furniture in the room, and it connected to a tiny windowless bathroom with a toilet and sink. There was a window in the bedroom, but it had bars on the outside, presumably to keep wild animals out of the building. It was now her prison.

She was terrified. How much longer did she have before the man came back and ended her life?

She started to pray.

SIXTEEN

Chris awoke to a dark-haired emergency tech checking him for injuries. He was still lying on the concrete, and his head was pounding. A dull, aching pain also radiated from his ribs and stomach, and shot throughout his chest with every breath he took. He raised his right hand to touch his head injury, and his fingers came away coated with his own blood. The moan came from his lips before he could stop it. The EMT pushed his hand away and continued with his assessment.

"Easy there, Agent. Welcome back. You took a nasty blow to the head, and have been unconscious for about ten minutes or more."

"I feel dizzy," Chris muttered as he tried to sit up.

The EMT pushed him back down and gently wiped away some of the blood from the head wound, then put some gauze over the area. Next, he pulled out an instant activation cold pack from his backpack and squeezed it to break the inner bag, then shook it before handing it to him. "That's not surprising, considering the size of the bump on your temple. Here, hold this on your head, and stay lying down. You could have a serious head injury. Do you feel nauseous?"

Chris shook his head slightly, regretting the movement as soon as he made it. "No, but I've got a massive headache."

The EMT nodded. "Also not surprising. Let me know if you experience any other issues. Your heart rate and breathing seem normal. We'll get you on a gurney in a minute and to the hospital so we can take some pictures of your injuries and see how serious they are."

Chris tried to sit up again, and this time pushed the EMT's hands away when he tried to stop him. "I can't just sit here. Where is Eleni?" Panic filled him as he looked around the area.

Two other EMTs were working on Zach Montgomery, who was also lying on the ground only a few feet away. Chris looked the other direction and saw Scarface's body still lying a few feet away from him. The Chicago Police Department had taped off the area, and he could hear a cacophony of sounds coming from the nearby street. Thankfully, the angle of the loading dock kept the onlookers away from the actual scene, but he didn't recognize any of the law enforcement officers that were working the area. He didn't see anyone from his office here yet either, but that didn't surprise him, since the Chicago PD would have been the responding agency. Somebody would notify the FBI, if they hadn't already, about his injuries. In fact, just as he was examining the faces of the police in the area to find one he recognized, one of the detectives came up and started asking him questions. He answered curtly, giving only the bare facts, so he could concentrate on getting the answers he needed from Montgomery. The man seemed satisfied and turned back to the other officers, while the EMT continued with his assessment.

"Does your chest hurt?" the dark-haired EMT asked.

Chris sucked in a breath when the tech touched his ribs. He hoped they weren't broken, but he didn't have time to find out. Eleni was nowhere to be seen, and dread and fear filled him in equal parts. Was she dead? Had he lost her forever?

He pulled free from the EMT, who complained, but didn't try to stop him, and moved over to Zach's side, pushing away one of the EMTs that was still trying to assess the other fallen man. "Montgomery, what happened to Eleni?" He noticed Zach's bloody shoulder, but he was conscious, and Zach met his eyes when Chris called his name.

"The guy with the gun took her," he said through gritted teeth, obviously in pain from the gunshot wound. "The one who shot me."

"Took her where?" Chris demanded.

"I'm not sure."

Another wave of dizziness swept over Chris and he put his hand on the building's wall to steady himself. He was struggling, but he couldn't stop—not while there was still a chance that Eleni was out there somewhere, still alive and breathing. Finally, when he had control of himself again, he took a deep breath and started again.

"Was she hurt?"

"Not that I know of."

"Do you know who the guy was who abducted her?"

Zach shook his head, his eyes miserable. "I've never met him before, but his name is Ramos. I don't know his first name. He's a local gun for hire. That's all I know about him."

"Why is your family trying to kill Eleni?" Chris finally asked, his tone exasperated.

Zach Montgomery grimaced, his expression one of deep pain and anguish. Chris could tell that the hurt the man was feeling was due to much more than just the bullet wound in his shoulder. He was obviously conflicted. It was written all over his face. "It's a long story."

"Well, I don't have time for a long story." He leaned closer. "Give me the highlights. Is she your sister?"

Zach hesitated, but finally nodded. "So, you know?"

"We weren't positive, but it sure looked that way."

Zach closed his eyes for a moment. "How'd you find out?"

Chris gritted his teeth, impatient. "We found an old album with her mother's things. It had some newspaper articles inside that described the kidnapping." He touched Zach's good arm to get him to open his eyes again. "I have to find her before that guy kills her, if he hasn't already. I need your help." He bent down on his haunches so he could be closer to Montgomery, whose voice was wavering with each exchange. The position ended up hurting him, though, and he opted to just sit on the concrete next to the fallen man.

Thoughts flowed through Chris's mind as he tried to make sense of what he had discovered, and what he needed to do next to save Eleni. He didn't have a lot of options, or time for guessing games. What he needed was answers. "Somebody from your family must have hired that guy to hurt Eleni." He leaned closer. "Was it you?"

"No," Zach said quickly. "I would never do that. I've been trying to protect her."

Outrage swelled in his chest. "Protect her? I've seen you stalking her!"

Zach tried to sit up to argue, but the EMT pushed him back down.

"Lie still!" the EMT ordered.

"I was trying to watch out for her," Zach declared, his voice clearly agitated. "I thought she was in danger, and I wanted to keep her safe. That's why I've been following her."

"Look," the EMT interrupted, clearly annoyed. "We've got to get him to the hospital. Now. If you want to interview him some more, you'll have to meet us at the hospital. You should be going there yourself to get your head and your chest checked out anyway."

Chris adjusted the ice pack on his head. "Can I ride in the same ambulance? A woman's life is in danger, and this guy is my only lead."

The EMT that had been working on Chris suddenly appeared back on the scene pushing a gurney, and the three EMTs worked together to get Zach Montgomery on it while Chris stepped back to let them work. Finally, the one in charge of the scene nodded. "I guess you can ride along, but we're leaving now. We need a surgeon to examine this shoulder wound and there's one already waiting at the hospital."

"Deal," Chris replied. He followed the group to the nearest ambulance, where they secured Montgomery in the back.

The dark-haired EMT helped Chris get up in the ambulance, and once he was seated, he removed the gauze from Chris's head, cleaned the wound again and then closed the damaged skin with butterfly bandages. "I get the impression you're going to refuse treatment at the hospital, so this will be a temporary fix. You could probably use some stitches, but the wound is in the hairline, so if you forgo the stiches, I doubt it will be noticeable once it heals."

"Thanks," Chris said as the other EMT in the driver's seat announced they were headed to the hospital and started the engine of the rig. A few minutes later, they were racing toward the emergency room. Chris called his office, and asked Caitlin to meet him there with a car. He hoped that whatever he learned from Zach, it would be enough to find Eleni and save her before the brute who'd taken her decided to end her life.

"I heard what you said," the Bears fan repeated. "But you're not listening to me. The price just doubled. If you want the woman, you're going to have to pay me what's right. I'm the one who has her locked safely away. If I don't get my money, and I mean all of it, then you don't get the woman."

Eleni listened carefully at the door, able to make out

her abductor's side of the conversation quite clearly. The walls of this shack were thin and the building was small. But even though her kidnapper's conversation had been going on for a few minutes, she still hadn't been able to identify the name of the person he was talking to, so she pressed her ear closer to the door, hoping somehow the name would be mentioned.

Was Zach Montgomery the one who set all of this in motion? She wasn't sure what to think, and her mind went back and forth as she thought through everything that had happened recently. He'd been present at the scene for most of the horrible events in her life over the last few days, and seemed to be pursuing her. Yet on the loading dock, he had jumped in front of the bullet that was meant for her. That action had probably saved her life. Had he survived after being shot? He'd fallen to the ground, but she had been pulled away so quickly she hadn't even had a chance to check on him. She hoped he was still alive.

Why would he do such a thing and take such a risk if he wanted her dead? And why would he want her dead in the first place? She had so many questions, and the pieces just weren't fitting together in her brain. She tried to focus on thinking through her past and searching for answers, but her mind kept floating back to Katie. She was so worried about her little girl. Who would help her with her homework? Who would cheer for her when she graduated from high school and college? Who would take her shopping for her wedding dress?

"Well, you'll just have to think about it, then. I'll

give you twenty-four hours. If you don't pay up before this time tomorrow, I'm telling her everything I know, and then dropping her off in front of a computer somewhere so she can write her next exposé. Your whole company will go down in flames, and you'll go to prison because you're too cheap to pay me what's right. But of course, that's entirely up to you."

His words gave her a small bit of solace. If the Bears fan was telling the truth, at least she had twenty-four hours or so left to live. But a lot could happen in a day.

Her thoughts strayed to Chris. The idea of never seeing him again squeezed her heart. She saw his smile in her mind's eye, and his gentle mannerisms and quiet strength. He was one of a kind. She would always miss Charlie, but even though she had vowed never to date again, with Chris, the idea actually seemed possible. Despite their vow to stay friends and friends alone, she couldn't fight the attraction that had continued to build between them, and the excitement she felt whenever she was around him.

She was in love with him, and had never gotten the chance to tell him what she felt. She didn't even know if he felt the same. After all, they had both said that friendship was all that they wanted, and Chris was dealing with a lot of pain and angst from his job. He'd made it clear he wasn't looking for a girlfriend or any sort of relationship.

Still, she couldn't deny how she felt. It had taken her a while to recognize and admit those feelings, and now that she had, the burning in her heart intensified. Somehow, she had to survive this ordeal, and make it back to the people she loved, even if friendship was all that ever existed between her and Chris.

SEVENTEEN

"I still don't understand why your family wants to kill Eleni Townsend," Chris told Zach as the ambulance continued on its way. "Why is she a threat to you?"

"Earl Montgomery, my father, never gave up hoping that his missing daughter would be discovered alive, even though she was officially declared dead a few months after she disappeared. He hired countless investigators over the years, but they all came up with nothing. My parents never had any more children, and they always wanted to know what happened to their little girl. Then, a little over a year ago, one of the investigators he hired found some articles written by Eleni Townsend, and thought there might be a resemblance to the age-progressed photo we have of her. Although we didn't know it at the time, Wesley Montgomery, my uncle, paid the same investigator to report anything he found to him that he also reported to my father." He paused and took a breath. "I can't prove it, but a year or so ago, I think Wesley paid a guy to kill Eleni and her family. He wanted to make sure that if Eleni was related to the Montgomerys, that the connection was never discovered. The job got botched, and only Eleni's husband died, and Earl never knew anything about the death, or the possibility that Eleni could be his child. Apparently, Eleni and her daughter were supposed to be in the car that night, too, but for some reason, it was only her husband." Zach moved uncomfortably on the gurney, his shoulder obviously still hurting him despite the pain medication that was flowing through the IV. "The police labeled Charlie Townsend's death a car accident, and the investigation didn't go very far, but Eleni was still out there." He swallowed.

"But why kill her? It doesn't make any sense!" Chris proclaimed. "She didn't even know about the connection. Her adoptive mother never told her about her past."

"Wesley couldn't take the chance," Zach replied.

He coughed, and the EMT got exasperated. "Can't this wait?"

"No," both Chris and Zach responded together, and then Zach continued, "Eleni is an heir to the company. Her kidnapping didn't change that. Even though she was believed dead, her death was never confirmed. Without that confirmation, there was still a threat to the future of the family company, at least in Wesley's mind. Wesley let it go when the first attempt to kill her got botched, but then my father died. Earl was the CEO of Montgomery Investments and wielded a lot of power—power that Wesley wanted. Up until his death, my father ran the show, and made it into the multimillion-dollar business it is today, and Wesley was always jealous and trying to take control. When Earl died, controlling interest of the company was split equally between Wesley and me. We have equal shares of the equity, but even though he's the CEO, I have veto power." Zach took a moment to catch his breath, then continued, "For the most part, I just stay out of his way. He can be a nasty adversary, and I never wanted to give him reason to have me eliminated. He also has several board members in his pocket, which would make challenging him very difficult. Wesley relaxed a bit once he got the CEO position, but my father never gave up looking for his daughter before his death, and always hoped that somehow, she had survived. Before he died, he put a special provision in the bylaws of the company that gave Eleni and me a controlling interest together, if she was ever found. We could leave Wesley as the head, or we could take it over and run it ourselves, but at least we would have the choice. Without those extra shares, I don't have enough power to oust Wesley from the CEO position, but with them, I can have him removed."

"Did you want to take over?"

"I didn't. I was happy with the vice president role and I have a nice work-life balance. But that was before I found out Wesley was hunting for Eleni again and trying to kill her. I don't know for sure, but I think her recent exposé brought up all of those concerns he'd had in the past. He wants to make sure he can remain in power, and that she'll never come forward and threaten his position." He shuddered. "I don't know Eleni. But she is my sister. I don't want her dead."

Chris shook his head. "So basically, this is all about money?"

"Basically," Zach replied. "Wesley will stay CEO, unless Eleni is found. If she is discovered, a DNA test will be done, and then Eleni and I would take over Montgomery Investments."

Chris tilted his head. "So how did Wesley make sure that Eleni was related? I mean, an old age-progressed photo is pretty flimsy evidence. I doubt he would go to all of this trouble on a hunch."

"You're right. He hired someone to break into their house a few months ago to obtain a DNA sample, and he confirmed the truth. Eleni Townsend is really Celia Montgomery. But he kept the information secret so he could keep the CEO position. I happened to come across the payment for the test, and secretly ordered a second copy of the report. That's what alerted me to what was going on." Zach sighed. "Then I overheard Wesley plotting to kill Eleni and Katie on the telephone, and I found the paper trail that showed how he hired Henry Jackson from Chicago to poison both of them."

Chris shook his head. "Why did he choose poisoning at a restaurant salad bar? There was so much collateral damage! He killed and hurt a lot of people."

Zach pursed his lips. "Wesley is not a straightforward guy. He thrives on intrigue. I overheard him say that he believed the poisoning would be thought to be a terrorist act or arbitrary at a minimum and, therefore, the crime would never point back to him, even if Jackson got caught. He also thought the investigation would go nowhere if there were several possible victims instead of just two." He sucked in a breath. "I found out about what he had hired Jackson to do, but not in time to stop him. By the time I got to Chicago, Jackson had already dispersed the poison, and Eleni and Katie were in the hospital. I went to the emergency room to check on them, and have been trying to keep an eye on her ever since."

"You know Jackson is dead, right?"

"Of course I know!" Zach said vehemently. "Wesley had Jackson killed to clean up any loose ends. Then he hired new people to try to kill Eleni. I've been trying to protect her as much as I can, but I have a hard time getting information in real time. Wesley is not a stupid man. In fact, he's one of the smartest men I've ever known, and he's gotten really good at covering his tracks."

"Well, why didn't you just go to the police?" Chris asked. He was having a hard time keeping the anger out of his voice. Here was a man who knew someone was in danger, but who never reported it.

"Wesley doesn't know I know. If he did, I'd be dead now, too. I've been walking a tightrope with him ever since my father died. Wesley is willing to do anything to make sure Eleni's connection to the family will never be discovered." Zach ran his tongue over his teeth. "What could I report anyway? Wesley has done an amazing job of concealing any information he's discovered. I really came across all of this by accident. All I could do was try to protect her from afar, and hope it was good enough."

"Who was the guy who actually took Eleni from the loading dock? That's what I really need to know. I have to find him before he hurts or kills her."

"I told you the man's name is Ramos. That's really all I know, but he must have been hired by Wesley."

"How do I find him?"

"I have no idea. I've been following Eleni around because I didn't know exactly what to expect or when her life would be threatened. I hoped if I stayed close enough, I'd be able to keep her safe."

Chris fisted his hands, frustrated. "There has to be a money trail somewhere to follow."

"True," Zach acknowledged. "But I usually find them after the fact."

The ambulance pulled into the hospital bay for the emergency room, and Chris grasped Zach's hand and put his card in it. "Thanks for everything you did. Here's my contact information. If you think of anything else, anything at all, please call me."

Zach nodded and met Chris's eyes. "Keep her safe. Please."

"I will," Chris promised as they took Zach out of the ambulance and wheeled him toward the hospital doors.

Now he just had to figure out how to keep that promise.

Eleni paced back and forth in the small room, then examined the window once again. It was painted shut, and when she pulled on it, nothing budged. Even if she was able to get it open, the bars looked like they had been securely fastened to the house, and she saw no signs of rust or other hints of weakness to give her hope that she could escape through the opening. Still, she had to try. It was really her only option. There was nothing in the bathroom besides the toilet and sink, and the bedroom was bare as well. The lock on the door was a dead bolt that locked from the outside, and she saw no way out through the door unless her kidnapper or someone else opened it. She was sure that if she tried kicking it or making other noises, her punishment would be swift and fierce. She moved back to the window and continued picking at the paint, hoping she could at least get the window open so she could take a better look at those bars.

She stopped for a moment and rubbed her arms, thankful that she'd worn a sweater today, as well as her jeans and tennis shoes. It was dark outside, and quickly getting cooler, and the cabin didn't appear to have any heat. It was going to be a long night.

She hadn't heard any more noise from the other part of the cabin for about an hour or so, and she wondered if her captor was still there or if he was out reconnoitering the area. Either way, she was glad to be away from him. He had a coldness in his eyes and the bearing of someone who just didn't care about those around him. Quite frankly, he scared her right down to her toes. She didn't think talking to him would convince him to change his plans. He'd already made it quite clear that he had no intention of holding a conversation with her. He wanted his money. Period. Her life meant nothing to him either way. She had to stay at the top of her game and wait for any opportunity to escape. She had too much to live for, and no one to depend upon to help her except herself.

That was wrong. God was always with her, and she could do all things through Christ who strengthened her. She stopped picking at the window and just prayed, laying out her fears and asking for God to watch over her child, Chris and her newly discovered brother.

Footsteps suddenly sounded in the living room of the cabin, and she tensed, waiting to hear which direction he was moving. He was coming to her room! She instinctively backed into the corner, the farthest she could get away from him. The lock clicked as he opened it, and then he opened the door.

He was a big man, and he filled the door frame with his bulk. He was still wearing the same Bears sweatshirt and jeans, but this time she actually noticed the gun he wore at his hip and the knife in the scabbard next to it. His eyes scanned the room and saw the damage she had done to the window, but all he did was shake his head. Apparently, he didn't believe she could escape that way either. His cold brown eyes moved to her and raked her up and down. Then he started walking toward her, a calculating grin on his face. He knew he was scaring her, and he was enjoying her fear. It was evident in his smile and the leer in his eyes.

He stopped right in front of her and bent his head

down so he could look directly into her eyes. She was already backed into the corner and there was really no place for her to go. She hated bullies, so even if she had to pay for it later, she steeled her spine and didn't back down or cower away from him, despite the fear that was pulsing through her veins. He was so close, she could smell the garlic on his breath.

He reached out and drew a finger down her cheek, and she instantly recoiled at his touch, despite her vow to stand up to him. "Hey, you're kinda pretty."

She slapped his hand away and put as much disdain as she could in her voice. "Don't touch me."

"Who's going to stop me?" he said with a laugh. "Come on now, don't be shy," he said, his voice husky. He moved his hand to stroke her hair that she had removed from her usual ponytail and was now hanging loosely around her shoulders. He played with the strands, letting them flow through his fingers.

"Your hair is beautiful—almost the color of my Blue Mountain coffee beans before I grind them." He grinned. "By this time tomorrow, I'll be able to travel and see where they grow that coffee firsthand. Pity you won't be able to travel with me. But you, my pretty friend, will be dead by then."

Eleni moved her head, pulling her hair out of his hand, and tried to get past him, but he moved with her, prohibiting her from escaping. He laughed again, but there was evil in his voice.

"And just where do you think you're going?" he said in a malicious tone.

Cold fear tightened a knot in Eleni's stomach as his malevolent eyes once again swept over her from head to toe. She knew, down deep, that she was in very deep trouble.

EIGHTEEN

Eleni's mind was frozen. She tried to think back to what she had learned in the self-defense class that she had taken a few years back, but fear and trepidation paralyzed her. What were the most vulnerable places to attack? They had gone over this in class more than once, but now, in the stress of the moment, she was struggling to remember the details. Eyes, knees, nose, throat, ankles, groin? Which was the best place to attack? Clarity suddenly came to her, and she used her head to hit him as hard as she could in the nose. He staggered back a step or two and he uttered a sharp curse, right before her second strike hit him hard in the Adam's apple, choking him. He instantly started gasping for air, and both of his hands went to his throat as if to protect it. For her third and final blow, she used her knee to kick him as hard as she possibly could in the groin. This attack brought him to his knees, and then he fell to the side, still struggling to breathe. A massive groan issued from his lips, but he still tried to reach for her, despite his obvious pain. She jumped back away from his groping hands and scooted across the bed, out of reach. Then she slammed the door behind her and locked it, trying to catch her own breath as the adrenaline pumped through her.

She was free for now, but how long would it last? The man was as big as a mountain and as strong as an ox. He was down after this round, but he would be back, and she knew she was far from safe. He would come back stronger and angrier. A locked door would only slow him down for a few minutes once he regained his equilibrium, but she was fairly certain he would break through it in no time. She had to make some decisions, and make them fast.

She glanced hurriedly around the room, looking for anything that could help her, but there wasn't much to see. A small desk sat against one wall, and she rushed over and searched the top, then the only drawer, hoping to find the car keys for the vehicle they had arrived in.

She found nothing useful. Papers, pens, and a few other odds and ends were scattered around, but she saw nothing that would help her. She imagined he still had the car keys in his pocket, and going back and trying to get them was out of the question. She knew they were out in the middle of nowhere. She turned and scanned the room again, this time searching for a phone—either a landline or a cell.

Had there been a cell phone strapped to his waist? She couldn't remember.

Suddenly, she heard movement in the bedroom, and the thumping noises spurred her into action. She had to get out of this cabin. Fast. She moved to the kitchen and frantically searched the drawers, finally pulling out a small flashlight from one of them and slipping it in the back pocket of her pants. It wasn't much, but it was all she saw that looked the slightest bit helpful.

She turned and glanced once more at the furniture in the living area, and her heart rate actually accelerated as she noticed the light catch a reflection on a black item on the end table.

He'd left his cell phone on top of a magazine, right next to a mug of coffee that still had steam escaping over the rim.

She said a quick prayer of thanks and grabbed the phone, then headed out the front door of the cabin. It was chillier than she expected and she rubbed her arms for a moment, then returned inside the cabin and grabbed a navy windbreaker she'd seen by the door. She didn't know how many miles it was to the nearest house, but anything that would help her keep warm would be a blessing if she was still traipsing through the woods all night. She quickly tied it around her waist so she wouldn't have to carry it. The noises in the bedroom were getting louder, and she dared not waste any more time before making her escape. She hurried out again, then jumped down the steps and ran down the driveway, grateful for the moon that was helping to light her way. She went about fifty feet, then veered into the surrounding woods, hoping that her captor would think she had stayed on the driveway and continue that direction when he started following her.

After running through the woods for a short distance, she paused a moment and checked the stolen cell phone, but as she had surmised, there was no service in this remote area. Her abductor must have used a Wi-Fi connection at the house, but she couldn't go back, not even to make a desperate call for help. Every second that ticked away could mean the difference between life and death. She pushed into the woods, darting around trees, bushes and overgrown weeds. Branches and brambles grabbed at her, and at one point, part of the windbreaker tore and she left a piece of fabric on the twig in her wake, but she kept going, pushing her body to her maximum endurance level. She had to escape before her captor caught up to her. If she didn't, she was as good as dead.

Despair welled in Chris's chest. Caitlin had met him at the hospital where he had promptly refused treatment, and they had headed back to the FBI building together where they were both searching frantically for any leads about Eleni's whereabouts. So far, they hadn't come up with anything, and he knew instinctively that they were wasting valuable time they just didn't have. They had contacted the federal prosecutor, but as Chris suspected, they didn't have enough for a search warrant at Montgomery Investments, and they were convinced that Wesley Montgomery would just request a lawyer and clam up if they tried to question him. In fact, if Wesley found out they were investigating his attempts to harm Eleni, Chris was convinced he would then destroy any evidence of his involvement, and maybe even speed up his orders to kill her. As Zach had claimed, the man was incredibly smart. They could move against him once they had Zach's help to find a paper trail, but that would take time.

They'd pulled the bullet out of the wall by the loading dock that had gone through Zach's shoulder, but so far, they didn't have any ballistic matches. And Zach was still in surgery and unable to answer any more questions, even if he did remember any more details that he hadn't already shared.

The name Ramos wasn't helping in the search. It was a very common name, and without more, there was no way to narrow it down to the man who had assaulted them by the loading dock. Chris had pulled up dozens of photos of men with that name that had been arrested over the years, but none had matched the features of the kidnapper.

What else could they do to find Eleni? How could they find one person in a city of well over two and a half million people? Chris and Caitlin both were completely out of leads and ideas. It was worse than looking for a needle in a haystack.

Caitlin drank the dregs from her coffee cup, then stood up and pushed away from her computer. "Okay. We've been at this almost two hours, and we still don't have any leads. I'm going to walk around and stretch my legs. I'll be back in five."

Chris nodded in acknowledgment but continued to stare at his computer screen without saying a word. They had discovered the identity of the man Chris had shot and killed during the abduction, but even checking his known associates hadn't given them a name or a place to search. The man wasn't even from the local area, and didn't have an address or any other ties to Chicago that they could investigate.

He rubbed his head that was still pounding from his injury, and swallowed hard, trying to keep his nausea under control. The ER doctor had not been pleased when he had left the hospital against medical advice, but he'd had no choice. He had to do everything he could to save Eleni. Still, this pounding headache and the roaring in his ears weren't helping him stay focused.

What was she going through? Was she already dead? His heart ached for her as he considered all of the possibilities. He'd been in law enforcement a long time. He'd seen the evil that men could do. He flashed back to when he had discovered the body of the little girl who had been kidnapped during his last case.

Was he going to lose Eleni, too? Was he going to find her lifeless body broken and beaten? A pain so deep it made him gasp spread instantly through his chest and made it hard for him to breathe. He pushed back from his computer and closed his eyes, trying to keep his hands from shaking.

He loved her. He didn't know when it had happened exactly, but he could no longer imagine a future without her. They had become friends, but even though they had both tried to deny it, the electricity of attraction had never dimmed between them. If anything, those feelings had intensified as they had gotten to know each other better.

What would he do if he lost her?

He didn't think he could bear it.

He fisted his hands and started to pray as strong emotions swamped him and made his muscles tighten involuntarily. The stress was nearly incapacitating. But God knew his heart. God would be with him to walk down this path wherever it led, and would never forsake him, or Eleni. He prayed for her safety, and for her to have strength with whatever she was facing. Then he prayed for God to strengthen him as well, and to help him stay focused.

His cell phone rang, breaking through the silence, and he opened his eyes and glanced at the screen. It said "Unknown Caller." He let it ring a couple of times, then decided to go ahead and pick it up. He didn't want to listen to another sales call, but he'd left several messages in his quest to find Eleni, and it was possible that the caller was returning his call and he just didn't recognize the number.

"Springfield, FBI," he answered.

"Chris! It's me! It's Eleni!"

He couldn't believe it. He was so stunned, it took him a moment to answer. "Eleni? Thank God you're still alive! Where are you? I've been searching for hours!"

"I'm out in the woods somewhere—southwest of the city, I think. This is my kidnapper's phone. Can you use it to find me? I had to walk for a long time before I found a signal."

Chris snapped his fingers and got his colleague's attention, then asked him to get Jerome Renfrew to trace the number and triangulate the location of the caller ASAP. Caitlin suddenly returned and he quickly got her up to speed. A moment later, he was back on the call with Eleni.

"Are you safe?"

"No, that guy is chasing me, I'm sure of it. He called someone and demanded more money, and was waiting to hear back about where to do the exchange if his offer was accepted. I managed to get away, but he's right on my tail."

"Is there anyone nearby that can help you?"

"I don't think so. I haven't even come across a house yet." There was a pause, and her voice took on a frantic quality. "Oh, Chris! I think I hear him! He's right behind me. I have to go!"

Eleni abruptly disconnected, and Chris's heart pumped a mile a minute as the fear swamped him. His muscles felt frozen, and for a moment, even his breath was caught in his throat. Was he going to be too late to save her?

Oh, dear God, help me! he prayed silently. *Help me find Eleni before it's too late, and keep her safe.*

A sudden sense of peace enveloped him, and his muscles seemed to start functioning again. He stood, motioning for his partner, Caitlin, to join him, and the two headed out to the parking deck. He couldn't lose her. If he did, he didn't think he could survive.

"I'm coming, Eleni," he said under his breath. "Just hold on. I'm coming."

NINETEEN

Eleni quickly stored the phone, then listened again to the sounds that surrounded her. She had thought she'd heard footsteps in the distance as twigs snapped and leaves rustled, but now she wasn't so sure. Was her abductor about to appear? Or was it just the wind and her active imagination? Her mouth seemed dry, and she swallowed convulsively, trying to catch her breath. Even her hands trembled, and she rubbed her clammy, sore palms on her jeans. She'd fallen twice in the dark so far but dared not use the flashlight she'd taken from the cabin, just in case it gave away her location. She was already worried that the noise she'd made with the call had drawn him closer. She listened carefully, hoping that her captor hadn't discovered what direction she'd fled.

She waited a few moments, but hearing nothing else, she continued her trek. She had been running for so long that her legs burned and felt like rubber beneath her, yet she had to press on. Images of Katie helped her stay focused, yet as she ran, images of Chris also appeared in her mind's eye. They gave her a feeling of warmth and comfort that she didn't expect but welcomed. She wanted to see both of them again. The thoughts and images drove her forward, even when she felt like she couldn't go on another step. She prayed continuously, asking God for the strength to make it to safety and survive this ordeal.

She suddenly heard running water, and was surprised a few minutes later to come across a stream that completely blocked her path. She still wasn't exactly sure where in Illinois she was and didn't recognize the area, but she was definitely thirsty, and took the opportunity to cup some water with her hands and quench her thirst. She glanced across to the other bank that was about twenty feet away, looking for any houses or people she could contact, but all she saw was more woodlands. She turned her attention back to the stream itself. The water didn't look too deep—probably three feet at its lowest point, so she started in, thankful for the tennis shoes she was wearing that protected her feet and gave her a slight bit of traction on the slippery wet rocks. The water was chilly and slowed her down, but also gave her body a chance to rest a little as she tried to choose the safest path across.

People liked living near water. The thought hit her when she was about halfway across the stream. Didn't real estate prices double if the land attached to a river or ocean? Did she have a better chance of finding help if she followed the water instead of heading back into the woods? It might be slower, but she might also have a higher chance of success if she changed her route. Speed was important, but so was finding someone that could help her. She finished crossing the water, but then slid into the edge of the woods and started heading downstream, hoping that the bushes and other vegetation at least partially hid her as she continued her trek.

She glanced behind her and, thankfully, still saw no sign of the man who had abducted her and brought her out to the woods. She had no illusions. He was back there somewhere, and wouldn't stop until he caught up with her again. She didn't know if he was following her on foot, or if he was scouring the countryside in his car, but either way, she couldn't let him find her. If she fell into his hands and couldn't escape again, a horrible fate awaited her.

She continued following the stream until her legs felt like gelatin and they just couldn't carry her another step. She had to rest, if only for a moment, and catch her breath. How long had she been walking since she'd talked to Chris on the phone? One hour? Two? Hearing his voice had definitely given her a second wind, but now she was tiring again, and didn't know how much farther she could go without a short break. She leaned against a tree for a moment and took the time to study her surroundings.

Was that a farm ahead? She suddenly stood up again and looked downstream more carefully. In the far distance, she saw some sort of light, and the shadows of what looked like two buildings. She squinted, trying to make out the shapes. Yes! There was a house and barn up ahead, and a small clearing illuminated by a light on a pole by the front of the barn. She didn't see any vehicles beyond a tractor under the light, but there could be something parked in the barn, or somewhere in the yard that just wasn't visible.

Renewed energy surged through her and she started again toward the farm, praying there was someone at home that could help her. Even knowing an address of the house would be helpful, and she could call Chris again and give him her location.

The woods continued for a short distance, but then thinned and finally gave way to a cornfield with young stalks standing about two foot high. She entered the cornfield, hoping she wasn't damaging the plants as she made her way toward the residence. The leaves were thick but the rows well-defined, free of weeds, and smelled of earth and freshness.

As she got closer to the farmhouse, she could see that both buildings had seen better days. The barn especially was weathered and leaning a bit to the right, and the house also had peeling paint and an unkempt appearance. Still, the house didn't seem abandoned. Curtains were visible in the windows, but Eleni didn't see any lights on inside. Either everyone was asleep, or they were away for the evening. An old porch swing startled her when it moved slightly in the wind, and she noticed two other chairs with faded floral cushions sat nearby, but no signs of life. She exited the cornfield and headed straight for the front porch of the house, hoping that even though she didn't see a vehicle, there was still someone home.

She made it up the stairs and raised her hand to knock on the red wooden door.

"That's far enough, don't you think?" the voice was quiet, but was filled with sinister amusement. The tone instantly sent a chill through her and her hands started to shake uncontrollably.

She turned slowly to see the Bears fan who had just come around the corner of the house. He had a malevolent smile on his face. "I figured you'd head here as soon as you took to following that stream. All I had to do was wait. There's not much else out in this direction." He took a step toward her. "Did you enjoy your walk through the woods?"

Fear gripped Eleni and her whole body started to tremble. She backed up a step, then another. The porch wrapped around the house, and the man was too close to the steps for her to go back down the way she'd come up. Her only hope was to get over the railing and escape to the barn. She backed up again, then put a leg over the railing and jumped.

Her abductor rushed to grab her, but she slipped away from him, barely dodging his grip. He got so close, she actually felt his fingers graze the fabric of her sleeve.

She ran toward the barn, not sure how she would evade him. She could hear him right behind her as she made it through the sliding barn door. She searched frantically around her, looking for anything she could use to protect herself. Her heartbeat tripled as his footsteps approached. She felt rushed and was close to hysterical. There was no time!

In contrast, her pursuer was calm and self-assured. In fact, she even heard him laugh. "You can't escape me. There's no place for you to go. Why don't you just give up and accept the facts? We'll enjoy some time together, and then we'll go for a little ride and you can pick your own burial site. I'll even let you dig the hole."

"Never," she said under her breath. There was no time to hide. She saw some farming implements that attached to a tractor and raced around them, trying to at least keep some distance from him, but she still saw nothing that she could use as a weapon.

"Why don't you just accept the inevitable?" he sneered. "You've made my life more difficult, but you can't escape your fate."

She suddenly spied a crowbar amongst the hay and dirt on the ground and reached to grab it, then turned to face him. *God, please help me!* she prayed silently. He was only about ten feet away now. She knew she probably wouldn't win this battle, but she was going to go down fighting. And she knew God was with her. Her terror was starting to ebb, and was replaced with an intense fierceness that strengthened her resolve. Regardless of how this turned out, she knew she wasn't alone. "I don't believe in fate. God is with me." She brandished the crowbar, even as he approached her.

"You think that little piece of metal is going to stop me?" he said, his voice rough and odious. "I always liked a challenge. Keep on fighting me. It will make everything more fun." He took a step toward her, then another.

Beads of perspiration popped out on her brow, and the metal felt slippery in her grasp. He was almost upon her, grinning like a Cheshire cat. Eleni forcefully swung the crowbar at him, trying to ward him off. Her makeshift weapon sailed through the air without making purchase. Then suddenly, she heard vehicles speed up and park outside the barn, then car doors slamming.

"Eleni?"

Relief so strong it was palpable swept over her from head to toe. It was Chris, and he wasn't alone. Three other FBI agents, all wearing the navy windbreakers with "FBI" emblazoned on the front and back, entered the barn.

Chris's eyes instantly took in the situation, and he pointed his drawn weapon at the aggressor's midriff. "That's far enough, Ramos. Freeze and put your hands up."

"You're not going to shoot me," the kidnapper said haughtily as he motioned with his hand. "You could miss and hit this pretty lady here."

Chris kept his aim steady and took a small step to the left. "There are a lot of things I'm not very good at, but shooting isn't one of them." He tilted his head. "I never miss."

Ramos laughed, then hurried to close the distance between himself and Eleni as he reached for her.

Two shots rang out, and thin wisps of smoke simultaneously came out of both Chris's and Caitlin's barrels.

The kidnapper looked surprised, then stared down at his chest, where two red circles were quickly expanding on his sweatshirt. He dropped to his knees, then fell forward into the dirt, face-first. He wasn't quite dead yet, and stretched out his arm, still trying to grasp Eleni, but she swiftly stepped back, making sure she was well out of his reach.

Chris rushed up to his side and took the man's gun from his waistband and secured it in his own, then flipped him over on his side so he could see his eyes. "Who hired you?"

The man didn't answer and Chris could see that he was fading fast. He gave him a little shake. "Who was it? Who hired you to kill Eleni?"

The man sputtered, but didn't say a word that Chris could decipher. Blood trickled out of the corner of his mouth and down his chin as he gripped Chris's arm. Then the light disappeared from his eyes once and for all and his hold loosened. His hand fell back and he died, right there on the barn floor. Chris reached for the man's neck to confirm his demise and felt for a pulse, but didn't find one. He readjusted his fingers, just in case, but still didn't feel a beat. He stood up, wishing things had gone differently, despite Ramos's violent and horrific behavior. He hated taking a life, but sometimes it was necessary, and the only way to stop someone who was bent on hurting others. He turned to Eleni, who readily stepped into his arms. The air felt thick, and he realized his hands were shaking.

"I was so afraid I'd lost you forever," he said softly, pulling her close. "Are you okay?"

"I am now," Eleni whispered back. "How did you find me?"

"We tracked the cell phone you used to call me. It was smart of you to make that call and leave the phone on so we could triangulate your location. I just kept praying that we would find you before the kidnapper did. I was so worried that we'd be too late."

Eleni tightened her arms around him. "You got here just in the nick of time. He would have hurt me, but he didn't. And now, I'm right where I need to be."

Chris pulled back a bit so he could see into her eyes, and smiled at the love he saw reflected there. His own heart was swelling within his chest as the relief swamped him. She was alive. He'd gotten there in time, and she had survived. He said a prayer of thankfulness and enjoyed the feel of her in his arms. She was soft and warm and made him feel whole. He relished the happiness that was budding in his heart for the first time in years. It was so foreign, he hardly recognized it, yet he grabbed ahold with both hands, never wanting to let the feeling, or the woman he was holding, go.

He glanced up around the barn, noticing that both Caitlin and the other FBI agent that had accompanied him had quietly left the barn. He knew they would be sweeping the area, and was thankful they had given him a moment alone with Eleni. He led her away from the body, then gently took her face in his hands so their eyes met once again. He drew his thumbs over her cheeks, barely able to believe that he had arrived in time and she was here, safely in his arms.

"I have to tell you something." He took a deep breath, then continued. "I thought I could be 'just friends' with you, like we talked about, but it's not possible. I love you. It's okay if you don't feel the same, but I had to tell you—"

She reached up and put a finger against his lips. "When I thought he was going to kill me, my biggest regret was that I hadn't told you I loved you." She smiled. "I didn't want to die without making sure you knew that. I love you right back."

He smiled, then leaned forward, gently placing his lips against hers. It was tentative at first, but then grew stronger as her words really sunk home. She loved him. Pure joy filled his heart until he thought it would burst. He laughed out loud and swung her around until she was laughing with him. God was good. All the time. He had brought Chris this amazing woman in his arms, and replaced the pain from his past with love.

EPILOGUE

As it turned out, the man who had been chasing her, scaring her, was actually her brother, and an innocent man as well. She smiled at him, thinking through how much her life had changed in the last couple of days. After Chris had rescued her from that barn in the countryside, she had been interviewed extensively by the FBI, and then gone straight to her friend's house to be with Katie and rest for a couple of hours. A quick nap and a shower had done wonders for her, and she was already starting to feel like her old self, despite the stress and emotional upheaval that had been her life for the past several days.

Eleni's next stop had been to go to the hospital to talk to Zach Montgomery. She'd had to wait for a while because he was still recovering from his surgery when she arrived. Once he was back in a regular room, they'd finally had a chance to talk, and Eleni was quick to thank him for taking a bullet for her on the loading dock. In return, Zach told her everything that he knew about her history and the previous attempts on her life. Then they spent several hours together, just talking and getting to know one another. Although she wanted to get to know her biological family, she was still a bit daunted by the possibilities. After all, her own uncle had been the one who had killed so many people in his attempt to eliminate the perceived threat that she and her daughter represented. Still, she couldn't be sorry that Zach would now be a part of her life.

She studied her brother lying in the hospital bed as Katie played Candyland with him on a board laid out on the hospital overbed table. A new DNA test had been rushed through and it was a match—confirming that she was the missing Celia Montgomery who had disappeared from that Jacksonville beach when she was three years old. Zach had informed her that Wesley had done a test surreptitiously before trying to kill her, but she'd wanted proof from a local lab, and it had substantiated her belief. Now that she'd gotten a good look at Zach, it was easy to see some resemblance as well. They both had the same shaped gray eyes and prominent cheekbones, and their hair was virtually the same color as well.

Eleni still had lots of questions, but right now, she just wanted to celebrate the fact that she was alive and Katie was back home. She was also excited to have a brother. She'd thought that when her mother died, she'd had no other family left, but now a whole new world and history had opened up to her.

She was conflicted about the feelings she had for her mother. She loved the woman and always would, but she couldn't help but wonder at her mother's role in the kidnapping when she was a child. Did she steal Eleni away from her biological family, or had that been someone else's doing? How did her mother even become her mother? She had dozens of questions that would probably never be answered. But she was an investigative reporter, so once things settled down and life got back to some level of normal, Eleni knew she would start researching so she could discover all that she could. Either way, Eleni realized she would have to come to terms with whatever her mother's role had been, and that if it was criminal in any way, she would have to forgive her mother for her actions. It would be a tough road to travel, but she had seen God do amazing things, and was sure He would also be with her during her search for answers.

"Do you know anyone named Joelle Wilcox?" Eleni asked.

Zach looked up from the game board. "Wow, that's a name I haven't heard in a long time. How do you know Joelle Wilcox?"

Eleni shrugged. "I don't, actually. I just found an old postcard from her in a memorabilia album that used to belong to my mother. The album was filled with clippings and other things about my kidnapping when I was three, so I thought maybe she was involved somehow."

"It's certainly possible," Zach agreed. "Although I was pretty young at the time, I remember Joelle was our nanny for about six months or so. I think she was actually our nanny right before that trip to Florida when you disappeared. She was caught stealing, so she got fired, and didn't make the trip with us. There was a big commotion about it, and I remember her shouting at my dad when he let her go." He shook his head, apparently remembering the scene. "She was really angry."

"Angry enough to try to pay your parents back by kidnapping their only daughter?"

Zach shrugged. "It's possible. We'd have to do some research. She may not even be alive anymore. I'm not sure what happened to her or even where she went to live after she left us."

Eleni filed that information away. If there was something to find, she'd do her best to discover the truth, but she wasn't going to let the past ruin her present, or her future. Her daughter's exuberant cry broke through her woolgathering, and she gave her an affectionate pat on her back.

"I'm almost at King Kandy's castle!" Katie exclaimed happily as she clapped her hands and moved her piece two purple squares forward.

Zach laughed. "How did you get so good at this game?"

"Mommy plays it with me a lot." She leaned closer as if they were sharing a big secret. "She lets me be the red player because red is my favorite color, and she's usually blue because that's her favorite color. Nobody ever wants to be yellow. We don't like that one."

Zach laughed again, then must have felt a pinch from his shoulder surgery. He rubbed his arm that was in a sling and ran his good hand up around the bandage that covered his injury. "Well, I'm glad she let me use the blue piece today. It was really nice of her to share. Blue is my favorite color, too."

There was a knock at the door, and Eleni turned to see Chris poking in his head. She waved him in. "How'd it go?" she asked.

Chris came fully into the room, then closed the door behind him. "Very well. Wesley Montgomery's arrest went smoothly. He lawyered up immediately. But we've got your kidnapper's phone showing their contact, that paper trail we found showing the payments Wesley made to Ramos and linking the two of them together, and Ron Harding's statement that Wesley approved the payment to Henry Jackson, as well as the receipt. I don't think the prosecutor will have any trouble proving his case."

Eleni blew out a sigh of relief. "That's good to hear." She glanced at her daughter. "I know I should have waited until I knew for sure that we were out of danger, but I just couldn't wait any longer before picking Katie up." She ruffled her daughter's hair affectionately. "I missed her too much."

Katie smiled up at her. "I missed you, too, Mama. I had fun with your friends, but it wasn't the same as seeing you every day."

Chris nodded to Zach. "We couldn't have arrested him without all of the information you provided on our way to the hospital. We would still be searching for answers without your help. I know that was tough on you, but I do thank you for your assistance, and for everything you did to keep Eleni and Katie safe."

Eleni reached over and took Chris's hand, then

gently led him closer to the hospital bed so he would feel more like part of the group. She met his eyes as the air crackled between them. She was in love with this big, shy, gentle man. He had done more than rescue her from that barn a few days ago when the killer had been about to strike.

He had broken through her barriers, and she was ready to put her fear and loss behind her and give love another try. She would always love Charlie, but she was finally ready to take another chance, and give Chris her heart. He had taught her that it was okay to trust again, and that she didn't have to do everything on her own. She wasn't a pro at these new lessons, but she was learning and growing. It wasn't an easy road, but there was no one else she would rather travel down it with. Somewhere along the way, Chris Springfield had stolen her heart.

"Did you get past Gumdrop Mountains?" Chris asked as he looked at the Candyland game. He gave Katie a smile and Eleni's heart skipped a beat as she watched their interaction. She knew he was still struggling when he was around kids. But she was confident that with God's help, they could help each other to overcome past hurts and forge a future together.

Chris gave Eleni's hand a gentle squeeze and felt an overwhelming rush of peace and happiness invade him. His chest felt tight, but it was a good and pleasant sensation. With God's help, he had brought this case to a successful conclusion, and that accomplishment had done much to restore his feelings of self-worth and contentment. He still wasn't sure if he was going to stay in law enforcement, but he had time to figure that out, and had decided to take a couple of weeks off to get his life back on track and determine God's will for his life.

He watched little Katie as she won the game against her new uncle and shone with enthusiasm. It was still hard to be around her, yet she was so vibrant and full of life that her happiness and zest were contagious. Despite his unease, he felt excited about the prospect of getting to know her as Eleni and he strengthened and grew their relationship. He had always liked children before that horrible case. Chris felt confident God would help him work through his difficulties.

He smiled at Eleni, and got an answering smile in return. She was so beautiful, so talented. Sometimes, he just couldn't believe how much God had blessed him by bringing her into his life. With God, all things were possible. For the first time, with Eleni by his side, he found his heart beginning to heal from all of the losses he'd suffered in the past.

Chris knew Eleni still had some decisions to make. Zach was poised to take over as CEO of Montgomery Investments, but he was committed to renewing his relationship with his sister. Eleni seemed excited about getting to know her new family—the family that had been stolen from her so long ago. Zach had offered Eleni a position in the company as well, but she had turned him down flat. She loved her job with the newspaper, and had no interest in changing professions. Chris loved that she was so passionate about her job, and hoped that as they grew even closer, some of that passion would rub off on him. Hopefully he would once again feel the fire that had drawn him into law enforcement in the first place. Even if it didn't, though, he knew that Eleni would be with him and would support him, no matter what he decided.

That was love. God had given him two precious gifts—Eleni and Katie—and Chris knew without a doubt that God would be with them, no matter what the future held.

* * * * *

If you liked this story from Kathleen Tailer,
check out her previous
Love Inspired Suspense books:

Under the Marshal's Protection
The Reluctant Witness
Perilous Refuge
Quest for Justice
Undercover Jeopardy
Perilous Pursuit
Deadly Cover-Up
Everglades Escape
Held for Ransom
Covert Takedown
Alaskan Wilderness Murder

Available now from Love Inspired Suspense!
Find more great reads at www.LoveInspired.com.

Dear Reader,

I was recently told about a boy, Jonathan Hagans, who went missing at the age of three during a family outing to a Florida beach back in 1968. The missing child was never found. Happily, in my book, I was able to bring about a somewhat positive outcome, yet as a parent of eight, I can't imagine the pain of losing a child, nor the agony of not knowing what happened. My research took me to the National Center for Missing and Exploited Children, and the problem was much bigger than I ever imagined. If this is an issue that concerns you as well, the National Center's website offers several ways to get involved to help the families dealing with a missing child: https://www.missingkids.org/

Thank you for reading my book. I truly appreciate you.

May God bless you!
Kathleen Tailer

Get 3 FREE REWARDS!

We'll send you 2 FREE Books <u>plus</u> a FREE Mystery Gift.

FREE
Value Over
$20

Both the **Love Inspired®** and **Love Inspired®** Suspense series feature compelling novels filled with inspirational romance, faith, forgiveness and hope.

HARLEQUIN
PLUS

Try the best multimedia subscription service for romance readers like you!

Read, Watch and Play.

Experience the easiest way to get the romance content you crave.

Start your **FREE TRIAL** at
<u>www.harlequinplus.com/freetrial</u>.